STORM TRACK

By Margaret Maron

Deborah Knott novels:

STORM TRACK
HOME FIRES
KILLER MARKET
UP JUMPS THE DEVIL
SHOOTING AT LOONS
SOUTHERN DISCOMFORT
BOOTLEGGER'S DAUGHTER

Sigrid Harald novels:

FUGITIVE COLORS
PAST IMPERFECT
CORPUS CHRISTMAS
BABY DOLL GAMES
THE RIGHT JACK
BLOODY KIN
DEATH IN BLUE FOLDERS
DEATH OF A BUTTERFLY
ONE COFFEE WITH

Short story collection:

SHOVELING SMOKE

MARGARET MARON

STORM TRACK

THE MYSTERIOUS PRESS

Published by Warner Books

A Time Warner Company

This book is a work of fiction. Names, characters, places, and incidents are either the product of the author's imagination or are used fictitiously, and any resemblance to actual persons, living or dead, events, or locales is entirely coincidental.

 Mysterious Press books are published by Warner Books, Inc., 1271 Avenue of the Americas, New York, NY 10020.

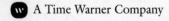 A Time Warner Company

The Mysterious Press name and logo are registered trademarks of Warner Books, Inc.

Printed in the United States of America

ISBN 0-89296-656-4

All chapter captions are taken from *The Complete Story of the Galveston Horror,* edited by John Coulter. United Publishers of America, © 1900 by E. E. Sprague.

For Sarah Nell Johnson Weaver:
First cousin, friend first

ACKNOWLEDGMENTS

As always, I am indebted to many for their help and technical advice, in particular: District Court Judges Shelly S. Holt, John W. Smith, and Rebecca W. Blackmore of the 5th Judicial District Court (New Hanover and Pender Counties, NC).

Belated thanks to Gail Harrell, Regional Library Supervisor of the Southeast Regional Library, who let me plug my laptop into her office socket when Hurricane Fran took away my electricity for a week.

Thanks also to Irv Coats, the generous and knowledgeable proprietor of The Reader's Corner, who always hands me the perfect source book.

Man is tinder, woman is fire,
and the devil is a mighty wind.

Attributed to St. Jerome

STORM TRACK

DEBORAH KNOTT'S FAMILY TREE

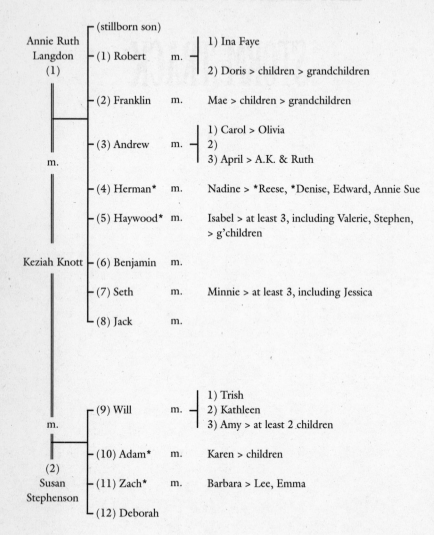

Annie Ruth
Langdon
(1)

m.

Keziah Knott

- (stillborn son)
- (1) Robert   m. — 1) Ina Faye
     2) Doris > children > grandchildren
- (2) Franklin   m.   Mae > children > grandchildren
- (3) Andrew   m. — 1) Carol > Olivia
     2)
     3) April > A.K. & Ruth
- (4) Herman*   m.   Nadine > *Reese, *Denise, Edward, Annie Sue
- (5) Haywood*   m.   Isabel > at least 3, including Valerie, Stephen, > g'children
- (6) Benjamin   m.
- (7) Seth   m.   Minnie > at least 3, including Jessica
- (8) Jack   m.

m.

(2)
Susan
Stephenson

- (9) Will   m. — 1) Trish
     2) Kathleen
     3) Amy > at least 2 children
- (10) Adam*   m.   Karen > children
- (11) Zach*   m.   Barbara > Lee, Emma
- (12) Deborah

*Twins

LATE AUGUST

Afternoon shadows shaded the dip in the deserted
dirt road where a battered Chevy pickup sat with the
motor idling. On the driver's side, a puff of pale blue
smoke drifted through the open window as the old
man inside lit a cigarette and waited. The two dogs in
back tasted the sultry air and one of them stuck its
head through the sliding rear window. The man
reached up and rubbed the silky ears.

A few minutes later, a green Ford pickup approached from the opposite direction and pulled even
with the Chevy. The old man acknowledged them
with a nod, then stubbed out his cigarette and
dropped it on the sandy roadbed.

"Evening, Mr. Kezzie," said the stocky, heavyset
driver who appeared to be in his early fifties. His hair
was thinning across the crown and his face was lined
from squinting through a windshield at too many
sunrises.

The other, younger man was probably early thirties.

He wore a neat blue shirt that had wet sweat circles under the arms.

Kezzie Knott peered past the driver. "This your cousin's boy?"

The older man nodded. "Norwood Love, Ben Joe's youngest."

"I knowed your daddy when he was a boy," Kezzie said, tapping another cigarette from the crumpled pack in his shirt pocket. "Good man till they shipped him off to Vietnam."

"That's what I hear." Norwood Love's jaw tightened. "I only knowed him after he come back."

And won't asking for no pity, thought Kezzie as he took a deep drag on his cigarette. Well, that part won't none of his business. Exhaling smoke, he said, "He the one taught you how to make whiskey?"

"Him and Sherrill here."

"I done told him, Mr. Kezzie, how you won't have no truck with a man that makes bad whiskey," his cousin said earnestly. "Told him ain't nobody never gone blind drinking stuff you had aught to do with."

"And that's the way I aim to keep it," Kezzie said mildly as he examined the cigarette in his gnarled fingers. There was no threat in his voice, but the young man nodded as if taking an oath.

"All I use is hog feed, grain, sugar and good clean water. No lye or wood alcohol and I ain't never run none through no radiator neither."

Kezzie Knott heard the sturdy pride in his voice. "Ever been caught?"

"No, sir."

"Sherrill says you got a safe place to set up."

"Yessir. It's—"

Kezzie held up his hand. "Don't tell me. Sherrill's word's good enough. And your'n." His clear blue eyes met the younger man's. "Sherrill says you was thinking eight thousand?"

"I know that's a lot, but—"

"No, it ain't. Not if you're going to do a clean operation, stainless steel vats and cookers."

He leaned over and took a thick envelope from the glove compartment and passed it across to Norwood Love. "Count it."

When the younger man had finished counting, he looked up at the other two. "Don't you want me to sign a paper or something?"

"What for?" asked Kezzie Knott, with the first hint of a smile on his lips. "Sherrill's told you my terms and you aim to deal square, don't you?"

"Yessir."

"Well, then? Ain't no piece of paper gonna let me take you to court if you don't."

"I reckon not."

"Besides"—a sardonic tone slipped into his voice—"there don't need to be nothing connecting me to you if your place ain't as safe as you think it is."

As Norwood Love started to thank him, Kezzie Knott touched the brim of his straw hat to them, then put the truck in gear and pulled away through August heat and August humidity that had laid a haze across the countryside.

Ought to've paid more mind to the noon weather report, the old man told himself as he headed the truck toward home. Thick and heavy as this air was, he reckoned they might get another thunderstorm before bedtime.

Automatically he took a mental inventory of the farm—not just the homeplace but all the land touching his that his sons now owned and farmed.

Cotton was holding up all right, and soybeans and corn could take a little more rain without hurting bad, but all this water was leaching nutrients from the sandy soil. Bolls was starting to crack though so it was too late to spray the cotton with urea to get the nitrogen up enough to finish it off. Tobacco had so much water lately, it was all greened up again. Curing schedule shot to hell. Just as well, he supposed, since the ground was so soggy along the bottoms you couldn't get tractors in without bogging down.

Playing hell with the garden, too. Maidie was fussing about watery tomatoes and how mold on the field peas was turning 'em to mush. That second sowing of butter beans won't faring so good neither—them fuzzy yellow beetle larvy making lace outen the leaves. Every time him or Cletus dusted 'em, along come the rain to wash off all the Sevin before it had a chance to kill 'em.

The boys was worried, but that's what it was to be a farmer. First you lay awake praying for rain, then you lay awake praying for it to quit. You done it 'most your whole life, he thought. All them years Sue tried to make you put farming over whiskey. Got to be a habit after a while. Certainly was for the boys.

And now another round of hurricanes setting up to blow in more rain?

Deb'rah won't going to be any happier 'bout more rain than the boys. She said she was about to get eat up out there by the pond. Fish couldn't keep up with the eggs them mosquitoes was laying in this weather.

Through the open back window, Ladybelle's nose

nudged the back of his neck. Kezzie took a final drag on his cigarette and stubbed the butt in his overflowing ashtray.

"Still don't see why she had to go and build out there when the homeplace is setting almost empty," he grumbled to the dogs.

CHAPTER 1

The situation . . . is portrayed day by day
exactly as it existed, and is not the product
of imaginings of writers who put down
what the conditions should have been; the
storm has been followed from its incep-
tion.

*August 31—Hurricane Edouard is now 31° North by
70.5° West. Wind speed approx. 90 knots. (Note: 1 kt. = 1
nautical mile per hour.) (Note: a nautical mile is about
800 ft. longer than a land mile or .15 of a land mi.)*

Math was not Stan Freeman's strongest subject. In
the margin of his notebook, the boy laboriously scrib-
bled the computations so he'd have the formula
handy:

90 kts. =
90 + (90 x .15) =

He rummaged in his bookbag for his calculator.
The fan in his open window stirred the air but did

little to cool the small bedroom. Perspiration gleamed on his dark skin. His red Chicago Bulls tank top clung damply to his chest. It'd been an oversized Christmas present from his little sister Lashanda, yet was already too tight. His distinctly non-stylish sneakers lay under the nightstand so his feet could breathe free. Three sizes in six months. After he outgrew a new pair in one month, Kmart look-alikes were all his mother would buy "till your body settles down."

At eleven and a half, it was as if his limbs had suddenly erupted. The pudginess that had lingered since baby-hood was gone now, completely melted away into bony arms and legs that stretched him almost as tall as his tall father. He was glad to be taller. Short kids got no re-spect. Now if he could just do something about his head. It felt out of proportion, too big for his gangling body, and he kept his bushy hair clipped as short as his mother would allow so as not to draw attention to the disparity.

At the moment, though, he wasn't thinking of his appearance. Using his light-powered calculator, he multiplied ninety by point fifteen, then finished writ-ing out his conversion:

$90 + (13.5) = 103.5 \ mph$.

For a moment, Stan lay back on his bed and imag-ined himself standing in a hundred-and-four miles per hour wind.

Freaking cool!

And never going to happen this far inland, he re-minded himself. He sat up again and picked up where he'd left off in his main notes: *Hurricane warnings posted from Cape Lookout to Delaware, but forecasters predict that Edouard will probably miss the North Car-olina coast.*

Gloomily, he added, *Hurricane Fran downgraded to a tropical storm last night.*

With a sigh as heavy as the humid August air the fan was pulling through his open window, Stan took out a fresh sheet of notebook paper and made a new heading.

NOTES—Meterolg

He paused, consulted the dictionary on the shelf beside his bed, tore out the sheet of paper and began again.

NOTES—Meteorologists say we're getting more tropical storms this year because of a rainy summer in the deserts of W. Africa. (Reminder—look up name of desert) (Reminder—look up name of country) This makes tropical waves that can turn into storms. At least they think that's what caused Arthur and Bertha so early this year.

He couldn't help wishing for the umpteenth time that he'd known about this new school's sixth-grade science project earlier in the summer. If he had, he might have thought about documenting the life and death of a killer hurricane in time for it to do some good. Unfortunately, nobody'd mentioned the project till this past week, a full month after Bertha did her number on Wrightsville Beach. Cesar and Dolly had been right on her heels, but both of them wimped out without making landfall.

Like Hurricane Edouard was about to do.

Just his luck if the rest of hurricane season stayed peaceful. When he came up with the idea of doing a day-by-day diary of a killer storm, Edouard was still kicking butt in the Caribbean and had people down at the coast talking about having to evacuate by Labor Day. Now, though . . .

He wasn't wishing Wilmington any more bad luck, but a category 3 or 4 hurricane would sure make a bitchin' project.

Sorry, God, he thought, automatically casting his eyes heavenwards.

"Son, I know you think you have to say things like that to be cool with the other kids," Dad chided him recently. "But you let it become a habit and one of these days, you're going to slip and say it to your mother and how cool will you feel then?"

Not for the first time, Stan considered the parental paradox. His father might be the preacher, but it was his mother who had all the Thou Shalt Nots engraved on her heart.

As if she'd heard him think of her, Clara Freeman tapped on the door and opened it without waiting for his response.

"Stanley? Didn't you hear me calling you?"

"Sorry, Mama, I was working on my science project."

Clara Freeman's face softened a bit at that. Guiltily, Stan knew that schoolwork could always justify a certain amount of leeway.

Yet schoolwork seldom took precedence over church work.

"Leave that for later, son. Right now, what with all the rain we've been having, Sister Jordan's grass needs cutting real bad and I told her you'd be glad to go over this morning and do it for her."

Without argument, Stan closed the notebook and placed it neatly on his bookshelf, then began cramming his feet into those gawdawful sneakers. His face was expressionless but every cussword he'd ever heard surged through his head. Bad enough that this wet and steamy August kept him cutting their own grass every week without Mama looking over the fences to their neighbors' yards. Sister Jordan had two teenage grandsons who lived right outside Cotton Grove, less than a mile away, but Mama could be as implacable as the Borg—which he'd only seen on friends' TV since Mama didn't believe in it for them. If ever she saw an opportunity to build his character through Christian sacrifice, resistance was futile.

Any argument and she'd be on her knees, begging God's forgiveness for raising such a lazy, self-centered son, begging in a soft sorrowful voice that always cut him deeper than any switch she might have used.

On the other hand, if he spent the next hour cutting Sister Jordan's grass, Mama wouldn't fuss about him going over to Dobbs with Dad this evening.

This was the second time they'd made love. The first had been in guilty haste, an act as irrational as gulping too much sweet cool water after days of wandering in a dry and barren land.

And just as involuntary.

Today they lay together on the smooth cotton sheets of her bed, away from any eyes that might see or tongues that might tell. Despite the utter privacy, and even though her mouth and body had responded just as passionately, just as hungrily as his, her lovemaking was again curiously silent. No noisy panting, no long ecstatic sobs, no outcries.

Cyl moaned only once as her body arched beneath his, a low sound that was almost a sigh, then she relaxed against the cool white sheets and murmured, "Holy, holy, holy."

"Don't," Ralph Freeman groaned. "Please don't."

She turned her face to his, her brown eyes bewildered. "Don't what?"

"Don't mock."

"*Mock?* Oh, my love, I would never mock you."

"Not me," he said miserably. "God."

She traced the line of his cheek with her fingertips. "I wasn't mocking," she whispered. "I was thanking Him."

Over in Dobbs, Dr. Jeremy Potts decided he'd put it off as long as he could. Having slept in this morning, he'd had to wait till late afternoon to go running. This hot and humid August had kept his resentments simmering. If not for the three biggest bitches of Colleton County, he told himself, he could be working out in the lavish air-conditioned exercise room at the country club instead of running laps on a school track under a broiling sun. He could follow that workout with a refreshing shower instead of driving back to his condo dripping in sweat. Thanks to his ex-wife who'd been wound up by her lawyer's wife, not to mention that judge who gave Felicia everything but the gold filling in his back molar, it would be at least another two years before he could afford the country club's initiation fees and monthly dues.

Thank you very much, Lynn Bullock, he thought angrily as he laced up his running shoes.

Jason Bullock hefted his athletic bag over his shoulder and paused in the doorway to watch his wife brush her long blonde hair. She had a trick of bending over and brushing it upside down so that it almost touched the floor, then she'd sit up and flip her head back so that her hair fell around her pretty heart-shaped face with a natural fluffiness.

"See you later, then, hon. I'll grab a hot dog at the field and be home around eight, eight-thirty."

"For the love of God, Jase! Don't I mean *any*thing to you?" Lynn asked impatiently, speaking to his reflection in her mirror. She pushed her hair into the artfully tangled shape she wanted and set it in place with a cloud of perfumed hair spray. "I won't be here later, remember? Antiquing with my sister? Her and me spending the night in a motel up around Danville? I can't believe you—"

"Only kidding," he said. "You don't think I'd really forget that I'm a bachelor on the prowl tonight, do you?" With his free hand, he stroked a mock mustache and gave her a wicked leer.

"And don't try to call me because we're going to ramble till we get tired and then stop at the first motel we come to."

It pleased her when his leer was replaced by a proper expression of husbandly concern.

"You'll be careful, won't you, honey? Don't let Lurleen talk you into staying somewhere that's not safe just because it's cheap, okay?"

"Don't worry. It'll be safe. And I'll call you soon as I'm checked in."

In the mirror, Lynn watched her husband leave. Not for the first time she wondered why she bothered to try and keep this marriage going. Except that Jason was going to *be* somebody in this state someday and she was going to be right there by his side. No way was she planning to wind up like her mother (after three husbands and five affairs, she was living on social security in a trailer park in Wake County) or Lurleen (only one husband but God alone knew how many lovers, one of which had left her with herpes and she was just lucky it wasn't AIDS). Besides, she'd busted her buns working double shifts at the hospital while Jase got his law degree so they wouldn't have a bunch of debt hanging over them when he started practicing. Now that the long grind was finally over, now that they could start thinking about a fancier house, a winter cruise, maybe even a trip to Hawaii, she wasn't about to blow it.

But that doesn't mean I've got to keep putting my needs on hold, Lynn thought, absently caressing her smooth cheek. Jase used to be such a tiger in bed. This summer, between long hours at the firm and weekends at the ball field or volunteer fire department—"building contacts" was how he justified so much time away—all he wanted to do in bed most nights was sleep.

Not her.

She took a dainty black lace garter belt from her lingerie drawer and put it in her overnight case. Black hose and a push-up bra followed. She dug out a pair of strappy heels from the back of her closet and put those in, too. Panties? Why bother? You won't have them on long enough to matter, she told herself with a little shiver of anticipation.

She thought about calling Lurleen, but her sister was going to Norfolk this weekend and wouldn't be home to answer the phone anyhow if Jase should call. Not that he would. He wasn't imaginative enough to play the suspicious husband. And no point giving Lurleen another hold over her. She already knew too much.

CHAPTER 2

The origin of a hurricane is not fully settled. Its accompanying phenomena, however, are significant to even the casual observer.

"C'mon, Deb'rah, we're one man short and what else you got to do this evening?" Dwight wheedled. "What's-his-face didn't change his mind and decide to come, did he?"

Sometimes Dwight can be even more exasperating than one of my eleven brothers. At least *they* like Kidd and Kidd seems to like all of them. Dwight's been the same as a brother my whole life—one of my bossier brothers, I might add—and he knows Kidd's name as well as he knows mine, but he'll never come right out and use it if he can help it. Don't ask me why.

Kidd Chapin's a game warden down east, Dwight Bryant is Sheriff Bo Poole's right-hand man and heads up Colleton County's detective squad here in central

North Carolina, so they're both law enforcement agents and they both like to hunt and fish and tromp around in the woods. There's no reason for them not to be friends. Nevertheless, even though they both deny any animosity, the two of them walk around each other as warily as two strange tomcats.

"No, he hasn't changed his mind," I said, with just the right amount of resigned regret.

Dwight would worry me like a dog at a rat hole if I gave him the least little suspicion of how sorry I'd been feeling for myself ever since Kidd called yesterday morning to say he couldn't come spend this Labor Day weekend with me as we'd planned. Kidd lives in New Bern, a hundred miles away, and we've been lovers for over a year now. But let his teenage daughter Amber crook her little finger and he drops everything—including me—to run see what she wants.

I know all about non-custodial angst. Not only do I see a lot of it when I sit domestic court, I've watched my own brothers struggle with their guilt. Hell, I even watch Dwight. Let Jonna call and say he can have Cal a day early, and what happens? Ten minutes after she hangs up, he's rearranged the whole department's schedule so he can head up I-85 to Virginia.

All the same, knowing about something in theory and liking it in practice are two entirely different things, and I was getting awfully tired of watching Amber jerk the chain of the man who says he loves me, who says he wants to be with me.

I brushed a strand of sandy blonde hair back from my face. It had bleached out this summer and felt like straw here under the torrid afternoon sun. When Dwight drove up in his truck, I'd been standing in the yard of my new house with a twenty-foot length of old zinc pipe in my hands.

"Here," I said, handing him the pipe. "Hold this and move back a couple of feet, would you?"

"Why?" he asked, as he held it erect and moved to where I'd pointed. "What are you doing?"

"Planning my landscape and I think I want a maple right about—stop!" I cast a critical eye on how the pipe's shadow fell across my porch. "Right where you're standing would be good. It'll shade the whole porch in August."

Dwight snorted. "It'll be twenty years before any tree's tall as this pipe. Unless you buy one with some size on it 'stead of digging a sprout out of the woods?"

Until the spring, my yard had been an open pasture with only a couple of widely scattered oaks and sycamores to shade a few of my daddy's cows. None of those trees shaded the two-bedroom house I'd had built on a slight rise overlooking the long pond. (A house, I might add, that was supposed to give Kidd and me some privacy. A supposition, I might add, we've had too frigging few weekends to test out, thank you very much, Amber.)

"I've already root-pruned six or eight waist-high dogwoods, three oaks and two ten-foot maples," I told him as I marked the spot where he stood with a cement block left over from laying the foundation. "Robert's going to take his front-end loader this fall and move them here for me. Want to come help me dig some five-dollar holes?"

He smiled at that mention of my daddy's favorite piece of planting advice: "Better to put a fifty-cent tree in a five-dollar hole than a five-dollar tree in a fifty-cent hole."

"Tell you what," Dwight bargained. "You play second base for me this evening and I'll come help you dig."

"Deal!" I said, before he could figure out that he'd just swapped half a Saturday of my time for at least two full Saturdays of his. "Give me ten minutes to wash my face and change into clean shorts. Make any difference what color shirt I wear?"

Back when I was playing regularly, the closest we came to uniforms was trying to wear the same color tops.

He turned around so that I could see JAILHOUSE GANG stencilled on the back of the red T-shirt that stretched tightly across his broad shoulders. (And yeah, long as I was checking out his back, I took a good look at the way his white shorts fit his backside.) Dwight's six three and built tall and solid like most of my brothers. Not bad-looking either. I can't understand why some pretty woman hasn't clicked on him and moved him on over to her home page before now. My sisters-in-law and I keep offering suggestions and he keeps sidestepping us.

"I brought you a shirt," he said, reaching into his truck for one like his.

I had to laugh as I took it from him. "Pretty sure I'd come, weren't you?"

He shrugged. "Been a couple of years since you played. Thought you might enjoy it for a change."

"So who're we playing?" I asked as I headed up the steps, already unbuttoning my sweat-drenched shirt as I went inside.

"Your old team." Dwight followed me as far as the kitchen, where he helped himself to a glass of iced tea from my refrigerator.

"The Civil Suits?" I asked through my open bedroom door as I stepped out of my dirty shorts and pulled a pair of clean white ones from my dresser drawer. There were enough law firms clustered around the courthouse in Dobbs to field a fairly decent team and I'd been right out there with them till I was appointed to the district court bench and decided I probably ought to step back from too much fraternization with attorneys I'd have to be ruling on. "They as good as they used to be?"

"Tied with us for third place," he drawled. "Today's the playoff. You still got your glove or do we need to borrow one?"

"I not only have it, I can even tell you where it is," I bragged. My sports gear was in one of the last boxes I'd hauled over to my new garage from Aunt Zell's house, where I'd lived from the time I graduated law school till this summer.

I found myself a red ribbon, and while I tied my hair in a ponytail to get it up off my neck, Dwight spent a few minutes rubbing neat's-foot oil into my glove. The leather wasn't very stiff. Half the time when they come over to swim in the pond, my teenage nieces and nephews wind up dragging out balls and bats. Just like their daddies—any excuse to play whatever ball's in season—so my glove stays soft and supple.

I poured myself a plastic cup of iced tea and sipped on it as we drove over to Dobbs in Dwight's pickup. He was going to spend the night at his mother's house out from Cotton Grove and since neither of us had plans for later that night, there was no point taking two vehicles.

Our county softball league's a pretty loosey-goosey operation: slow pitch, a tenth player at short field, flexible substitutions. It's played more for laughs and bragging rights than diehard competition because the season sort of peters out at the end of summer when so many people take off for one last weekend at the mountains or the coast. Instead of a regulation field, we play on the new middle school's little league field where baselines are shorter.

For once, Colleton County's planners had tipped a hat to environmental concerns and hadn't bulldozed off all the trees and bushes when they built the new school. They'd left a thick buffer between the school grounds and a commercial zone on the bypass that lies north of the running track. Mature oaks flourished amid the parking spaces and a bushy stand of cedars separated the parking lot from the playing field.

Dwight's team, the Jailhouse Gang, are members of the Sheriff's Department, a couple of town police officers, a magistrate and some of the clerks from the Register of Deeds's office.

The Civil Suits are all attorneys with a couple of athletic paralegals thrown in, and sure enough, Portland Brewer called to me as I was getting out of Dwight's truck.

"Hey, Deborah! Whatcha doing in that ugly red shirt?"

Portland's my height, a little thinner, and her wiry black hair is so curly she has to wear it in a poodle cut that makes her look remarkably like Julia Lee's CoCo.

We've been good friends ever since we got kicked out of the Sweetwater Junior Girls Sunday School Class one Sunday a million years ago when we were eight. Her Uncle Ash is married to my Aunt Zell, which also makes us first cousins by marriage.

Back when I was on the verge of messing up my life for good, I noticed that Portland was the only one of the old gang who seemed to be loving her work. It wasn't that I had this huge burning desire to practice law. No, it was more like deciding that if she could ace law school, so could I. She snorts at the idea of being my role model, but I laugh and tell her I'm just grateful she wasn't happily dealing dope back then or no telling where we'd've both wound up.

"Cool shirts," I said when Dwight and I caught up with her and her husband Avery, who's also her partner in their own law firm.

Their T-shirts didn't have the team's name on the back, but they *were* printed to look like black-tie dinner jackets, if you can picture dinner jackets with short sleeves. Black shorts completed an appearance of wacky formality that was a little disconcerting when they joined us down the sidelines for throwing and catching practice while a team from the fire department and faculty members from the county schools battled it out on the field.

I was rusty with my first few throws, but it's like riding a bicycle. Before long, I was zinging them into Dwight's glove just like old times when I was a tagalong tomboy and he'd drop by to play ball with my brothers.

I was soon just as hot and sweaty as back then, too,

and more than ready to take a break when someone showed up with the team's drink cooler.

Quite a few people had come to play and were either waiting to start or still hanging around after their own games. There were also forty or fifty legitimate spectators in the stands, and among the kids who stood with their noses to the wire behind home plate, I recognized Ralph Freeman's son Stan.

Ralph was called to preach at one of the black churches this past spring, but Balm of Gilead is in the midst of a major building program and membership drive and they can't afford to pay him a full-time minister's salary yet. In addition to his pastoral duties, he was going to be teaching here at the Dobbs middle school, and I wasn't surprised to see him out on the field with other Colleton County teachers.

"Who's ahead?" I asked Stan. "And what inning is it anyhow?"

"Dad's team's up by six," he said with a smile as wide as Ralph's. "Bottom of the fifth."

So it'd be another two innings before our game started, and the way both pitchers were getting hammered, it could be six or six-thirty.

By now, the westering sun sat on a line of thin gray heat clouds like a fat red tomato on a shelf, a swollen overripe tomato going soft around the edges. All this heat and humidity made it look three times larger than usual against a gunmetal gray sky. The air was saturated with a warm dampness. Any more and it'd be raining. A typical summer evening in North Carolina.

Portland's team and ours clustered loosely on the bleachers near third base and we sounded like a PBS fund-raiser the way all the pagers and cell phones kept going off. I hadn't brought either with me since I had no underlings and was no longer subject to the calls of clients, but Dwight had to borrow Portland's phone twice to respond to his beeper. Both were minor procedural matters.

Jason Bullock was on the row behind me and his phone went off almost in my ear. Nice-looking guy in an average sort of way. Mid-twenties. Brown hair with an unruly cowlick on the crown. He's so new to the bar that the ink on his license is barely dry. He's only argued in front of me four or five times. Seems pretty sharp. Certainly sharp enough that Portland and Avery had taken him on as a junior associate. I didn't know his marital status, but I figured he was talking to either his wife or live-in.

I heard him say, "Hey, honey. Yanceyville? Already? You must've made good time. Didn't pick up another speeding ticket, did you? . . . No, looks like our game's going to run late. We haven't even started yet, so I'll be here at least another two hours. . . . Okay, honey. Any idea what time you'll be home tomorrow? . . . Yeah, okay. Love you, too. . . . Lynn? *Lynn?*"

Beside me, Portland turned around to ask, "Something wrong?"

"Not really. She hung up before I thought to ask her what motel she's at. She and her sister have gone antiquing up near the Virginia border."

"I didn't realize Lynn was interested in antiques," said Portland, who'd rather poke through junk stores and flea markets than eat.

"Yeah, she'd go every weekend if she could. She loves pretty things and God knows she's earned the right to have them. Not that she buys much yet. But she says she's educating her eye for when we can afford the real things."

"Take more than a few antique stores to educate *that* eye," Portland murmured in my ear when Bullock got up to stretch his legs.

I raised my eyebrows inquiringly, but for once Portland looked immediately sorry she'd been catty.

"Jason's smart and works hard," she said. "Lynn, too, for that matter. He'll probably be a full partner someday."

In other words, it's not nice to be snide about a potential partner's wife.

"Why are all the cute ones already married?" sighed one of the Deeds clerks on the row in front of us as she watched Bullock walk toward the concession stand.

"Because they get snagged early by the trashy girls who put out," said her friend.

"Trashy?" I silently mouthed to Portland, but she just shook her head and said, "So where's Kidd? I thought he was coming this weekend."

"Me, too."

She immediately picked up on my tone. "Y'all didn't have a fight, did you?"

I shook my head.

"Come on, sugar. Tell momma."

So we moved up and back a few bleacher rows away from the others where we wouldn't be overheard and I spent the next half-hour unloading about Amber and how she seemed to be trying to sabotage my relationship with Kidd.

"Well, of course she is," Portland said. "You're a

threat to the status quo. She's what—sixteen? Seventeen?"

"Sixteen in October."

"Give her till Christmas. Once she gets her driver's license and a taste of freedom, she'll be more interested in boys than her father."

"Don't count on it," I said bitterly. "It just hurts that Kidd can't see how she's manipulating him."

"You haven't said that to him, have you?"

I shook my head. "I'm not that stupid."

"Good. He may be subconsciously putting the father role above the lover, but you don't want him making it a conscious choice."

"I *said* I wasn't that stupid," I huffed. "I do know that if it's a choice between Amber and me, I'll lose. I just wish he could understand that he doesn't have to choose. I'm willing to take my turn, but she wants her turn and mine, too, and he has to start thinking more about *my* needs once in a while."

"Oh, sugar," Portland said, squeezing my hand. "Just keep thinking license, license, license."

I gave her a rueful smile and promised I would. Portland likes Kidd fine, but what she really likes is the idea that he might be for me what Avery is for her, somebody to love and laugh with and keep warm with on cold winter nights.

Despite the still evening air, the smell of popcorn and chopped onions floated up to us as the sun went down. People were coming and going with hot dogs so we succumbed to the temptation of one "all the way." Here in Colleton County, that's still a dog on a bun with chili, mustard, coleslaw and onions. Enough Yankees have moved in that some of us've heard about sauerkraut on hot dogs, but Tater Ennis, who runs the concession stand, doesn't really believe it's true and he certainly doesn't sell it.

As we waited in line, I was surprised to suddenly spot Cyl DeGraffenried, an assistant DA in Doug Woodall's office, among the spectators. Cyl is most things black and beautiful, but I've never heard of any interest in sports. In fact, in the three years she'd been on Doug's staff, this was the first time I'd seen her at a purely social community gathering with no political overtones. She's the cat who walks alone and her name is linked to no one's.

While I watched, Stan Freeman stopped in front of her, and from their body language I could tell that they were having the same conversation he and I'd had earlier. He pointed to his father out on the field and I saw her nod. After the boy moved on, I tried to see who she was there for—volunteer fireman or school member—but she didn't cheer or clap so it was impossible to know even which team, much less which man.

"Is Cyl seeing someone?" I asked Portland.

She shrugged, as ignorant as me.

("As *I*," came the subliminal voice of my most pedantic high school English teacher. "As is not a preposition here, Deborah, and it *never* takes an objective pronoun.")

More friends and relatives, teenage couples looking for a cheap way to spend the evening, town kids and idlers began to trickle into the bleachers through an opening in the shrubbery that surrounded the parking lot. School had opened last Monday and this was day one of the Labor Day weekend, the last weekend of

long lazy summer nights. Our weather would probably stay hot on into early October, but psychologically,
summer always feels over once school starts and Labor
Day is past.

A few families had spread blankets on the grass out
beyond the centerfield fence where they could picnic
and let their children run around while watching the
game, and several hardy souls were even jogging along
the oval track that circles next to the trees bounding
the school's perimeter. As I munched on my hot dog,
it made me hot just to watch them.

Coming down the homestretch was a man dressed
in one of those Civil Suit T-shirts, but at that distance,
I couldn't make out his face under his black ball cap.

"Millard King," said Portland when I asked.

"That's Millard King? Last time I saw him, he was
carrying at least fifty more pounds."

This man was trim and fit.

Portland nodded. "Love'll do that."

"Who's the lucky woman?"

She shrugged. "Some Hillsborough debutante's
what I heard. Old money. Very proper. I think her father's on the court of appeals. Or was it the state
Supreme Court?"

The parking lot was gravel over clay but with all the
rain we'd had in the last couple of weeks, we didn't
have to put up with the clouds of dust that usually
drifted up over the tall shrubbery as cars pulled in and
out with some people leaving and more arriving.

The game in progress wound down to the last two
outs, and Avery and Dwight, the two team captains,
started counting heads and writing down the batting
order.

"Where the hell's Reid?" Avery asked Portland. "He swore he'd be here by five-thirty."

"Reid?" I asked. "Reid Stephenson's playing softball?"

Reid is a cousin and my former law partner when the firm was Lee, Stephenson and Knott, before I took the bench. He's the third generation of Stephensons in the firm and I was fourth generation because his grandfather was also my great-grandfather. (The Lee is John Claude Lee, also my cousin, but no kin to Reid.) Generationally, Reid's on the same level as my mother and Aunt Zell. In reality, he's a couple of years younger than I am, although John Claude, who's been happily married to the same woman for thirty-five years, has made it clear more times than one that he considers us both on the same emotional level.

That's not particularly accurate.

Or fair.

I think of myself as serially monogamous and I don't mess around with married men, but ever since Reid's marriage broke up, he seems to be on a sybaritic mission to bed half the women in Colleton County, married or single.

"Reid's always been a sexual athlete," I said. "That's why Dotty left him. But when did he take up outdoor sports?"

Portland laughed. "Back in July. Right after he pigged out at your pig-picking. One of the young statisticians in Ellis Glover's office said something about his cute little tummy and Reid signed up for our team the next day."

"Unfortunately, he still has his own idea of warm-up

practice," Avery said dryly. "And he never gets here on time."

Ralph Freeman's team held on to their comfortable lead in the bottom of the seventh and our game could finally get underway.

First though, each team had to line up at home plate and let the *Ledger* photographer take a group picture. The picture itself only took a minute, but we had to stand in place another five minutes while the photographer laboriously wrote down every name, double-checking the spelling as he went. He must've been reamed good by Linsey Thomas, the editor and publisher, who believes that the *Ledger* thrives because Colleton County readers like to see their names in print. *And* spelled correctly.

Dwight won the coin toss, elected to be the home team, and we took the field a little before six-thirty.

Colleton County is mostly sandy soil, but the ball diamond has a thick layer of red clay that was dumped here when the Department of Transportation widened the four-lane bypass less than a quarter-mile away as the crow flies.

With so much humidity, my feet soon felt as if I had about five pounds of clay clogged to the bottom of each sneaker, but that didn't stop me from making a neat double play when Jason Bullock hit a grounder through the box in the first inning.

Reid had arrived, cool and debonair, just in time to have his picture taken, but I didn't get to speak to him till the bottom of the second when I hit a double, then moved to third—Reid's position—on a pitching error.

He just smiled when I needled him about getting there late.

"Is she in the stands?" I asked. "Or doesn't she care for ball games?"

"Not *soft*ball games," he said with a perfectly straight face as one of the dispatchers popped up, leaving me stranded.

Top of the seventh, tied three all, and Millard King doubled to score Portland before we could get them out. Heat lightning flashed across the sky and there were distant rumbles of thunder. As shadows lengthened across the field, the floodlights came on. We were down to our last out when Avery walked me. Then Dwight stepped up to the plate and smacked the first pitch clear over the right field fence for the only home run of the game. I was waiting for him at home plate and gave him an exuberant hug.

A gang of us went out afterwards for beer and pizza—Portland and Avery's treat. Jason Bullock and one of their paralegals joined the two Deeds clerks who'd scored in the fifth inning, the dispatcher, Dwight and me. Everybody else, including my randy cousin Reid, pled previous commitments. Our waiter pushed two tables together and we sat down just as the rain started.

"They say Edouard'll probably miss the coast," Avery said as fat drops splattered against the window behind him. "Fran's still out there though."

Lavon, the small trim dispatcher, said, "And Gustave's tooling along right in behind her."

"I'm real mad at Edouard," said the paralegal (Jean? Debbie?), giving him a pretty little frown. "I bought me a brand new bikini to wear to the beach this weekend but I was afraid to go with a hurricane maybe coming in. And then it blew right on past us so I stayed home for nothing."

I instantly hated her. It's taken constant vigilance to keep my weight the same as it's been since I was twenty, but even on my skinniest days, there's no way I'd ever have the nerve to wear a bikini in public.

Beneath her mop of tight black curls, Portland was looking indecisive, but not about bikinis. She and Avery have a condo at Wrightsville Beach and a small boat with an outboard motor for waterskiing and puttering around the shoals. "Bertha didn't hurt us, but if we're going to keep getting bad storms—?"

Avery nodded. "Maybe we'd better run down tomorrow, close the shutters and bring the boat back up here."

Our pizzas arrived amid trash talk and laughter as we rehashed the game. Jason jazzed me that he'd given me such an easy double play that I owed him a good decision on his next DWI defense. We didn't get into courthouse gossip till there was nothing left of our pizzas except a logpile of crusts. As I suspected, the paralegal had her eye on Lavon and cut him out of the pack as soon as we'd finished eating.

That broke up the party.

Rain was falling heavier as Dwight and I drove back toward Cotton Grove, with the taillights of Jason Bullock's car ahead of us all the way till we turned off onto Old 48 and he kept going on into town.

By the time we drove into my yard, the rain was coming down so hard that we sat in the truck a few minutes to see if it'd slack off.

"You were right," I told Dwight as rain thundered

on the truck roof. "Tonight was fun. I'm glad you asked me to fill in, but I have a feeling I'm going to be sore tomorrow."

"You probably ought to soak in a hot bath and take a couple of aspirin before you go to bed."

"Come in for a nightcap?"

"Naw, I'd better get on. Mother'll be expecting me."

He reached out and gave my ponytail a teasing tug. "Out there on the field tonight, with your hair tied up in that red ribbon, you looked about fourteen again."

I grabbed my glove, leaned over to give him a good-night kiss on the cheek, and opened the door.

"Deb'rah—?"

I looked at him inquiringly.

He hesitated, then turned the key in the ignition. "Let me see if I'n get a little closer to the door so you don't get wet."

"Don't bother." I opened the truck door wide and stepped out into the downpour. "Feels good."

I held my face up to the sky and let the warm rain pelt my face. I was instantly soaked to the skin with my clothes plastered to my body, but since I was going straight in the bathtub anyhow, what difference did it make?

"You're crazy, you know that?" said Dwight. "*And* you're getting my seat wet."

I laughed and slammed the door. He waited with the lights on till I dug the keys out of my pocket and let myself in the house, then gave a goodnight toot of his horn and drove off through the rain.

I'd forgotten to leave my answering machine on, so there was no way to know if Kidd had tried to call.

CHAPTER 3

Husbands lost their wives and wives their
husbands, and the elements were only
merciful when they destroyed an entire
family at once.

*September 1—Edouard missed us completely. Down from
a category 4 hurricane to a category 3, and heading out
to sea. (Note: Make a chart that shows all 5 categories on
the Saffir-Simpson scale.) Winds still up to 100 knots but
dropping.*

*Tropical Storm Fran reclassified yesterday as a hurri-
cane. 22°N by 63°W, winds at 70 knots and gathering
strength. Tracking west-northwest at about 7 mph. Tropical depression #7 has moved off the African coast out
into the Atlantic and is now called Tropical Storm Gus-
tav.*

Stan paused and compared his maps to those in the
newspaper. His were slightly more up-to-date because
the newspaper went to press with Fran's position as of

eleven p.m. last night, while he had the radio's report from only a few minutes ago.

The radio was old and the original aerial had long since been replaced by a straightened wire hanger, but it had shortwave capabilities and when atmospheric conditions were right, it really did pick up stations far beyond the range of his regular AM/FM radio and tape player. In bed at night, he kept it tuned too low for his mother to hear and he often fell asleep with voices whispering foreign languages past the static, into his ear. Spanish and French, and occasional bursts of Slavic or German, twined through his sleeping brain and dreamed him into worlds beyond Cotton Grove.

The radio had come into its own with this science project. Its weather band made keeping up with all these hurricane movements almost as easy as watching the weather channel on his friend Willie's television.

Too bad Mama was so against television, Stan thought wistfully. (And good thing she didn't know that this radio could pick up the audio of some local TV stations.) Still, it was sort of fun to pinpoint the storm's positions just by listening and to try and guess where they'd be at the next reading. Right now, if Fran kept going straight, it'd hit between Cape Canaveral and Jacksonville, yet forecasters were beginning to predict that it'd turn north before that and could make landfall between Charleston and Wilmington by the end of the week if it didn't get pushed out to sea sooner.

He read over the sheets he had photocopied from a reference book at the county library over in Dobbs before the ball game yesterday, then began to write again, conscientiously casting the information he had gleaned into his own words. Intellectual honesty was one of the few things Dad preached about at home and Stan frowned in concentration as he wrote, skirting that fine line between plagiarism and honest summation.

NOTES: Here's how tropical storms strengthen into hurricanes: Warm air rises, cold air sinks. Warm humid air rises from the tropical waters of the Caribbean. As it rises, the water vapor condenses and forms clouds. That releases heat, which warms the upper air around it and that makes the upper air rise even higher. More air [cooler] flows down to the water surface to replace the rising air [warmer] and that starts a spiral of wind around a center of rotation. These storm winds speed up as they near the eye and form spiraling bands. Each band is like a separate thunderstorm and the heaviest are the ones that surround the eye.

He had already begun to consider the problem of constructing a 3-D model of a hurricane. Bands of cotton arranged in spirals on top of a map of the ocean? Build up the Caribbean Islands with a salt and flour dough that he could paint green?

He scissored the weather map from the paper and dated it for his growing file of clippings, then neatly refolded that section and carried it back to the living room.

The house was wreathed in Sunday silence as he stepped into the hall. Dad would be thinking out tonight's sermon, Mama would be talking in low tones with her prayer partner at the dinner table or on the back porch, her Bible open between them. No sound from Lashanda's room. She'd probably fallen asleep on the floor in the middle of her dolls.

The carpet let Stan move so noiselessly that his father did not stir when he entered the room and laid the paper on the coffee table with the rest of the Sunday pile.

The big man's breaths continued deep and regular, never quite breaking into a snore, but heavier than if he were awake. The soft leather Bible lay open on the arm of his lounge chair. Several index cards had fluttered to the floor. Ralph Freeman seldom wrote out his sermons, but he did make notes of the points he wished to cover. Stan tiptoed closer to the lounge chair, torn between wanting to look on his father's face without being seen, yet feeling vaguely guilty at doing so.

Was this what the Bible meant when it condemned Noah's son for looking upon Noah's nakedness? Because even though Dad was certainly dressed in suit pants, white shirt and tie, there was something naked about his face with the lines smoothed out, his eyes closed, his mouth relaxed.

For one confused moment, Stan wished he were a little kid again so he could crawl onto that lap, lay his head against that crisp white shirt and hear his father's heart beating strong and sure.

Seeing him like this with all the tension gone out of his body made Stan realize how much things had changed since they moved to Colleton County this spring.

Especially in the last month.

And it wasn't just because Balm of Gilead had been burned to the ground six weeks after they arrived. The person who set the fire had nothing against them personally or the church either and was now locked up in a Georgia penitentiary. Dad knew before they came that he was called to help Balm of Gilead's congregation raise a bigger, finer church and he'd been excited about it. Made them excited, too.

Not Mama though.

She hated to leave Warrenton but she hadn't tried to talk Dad out of it when he brought it to family council. "I'm called to be your wife," she'd said. "If you're called to go down there, then it's my duty to go with you."

"I would hope it's more than duty," Dad had teased, but Mama hadn't smiled back.

"If we're moving, then I'd better get some boxes tomorrow," she'd said. "Start packing."

"If you don't want to do this, Clara, tell me."

"No, it's fine," she'd said.

Looking at his father's sleeping face, the worry lines smoothed out for the moment, Stan realized that it wasn't fine, hadn't been fine even before they left Warrenton. More and more, it was as if he and Dad and Lashanda were in a circle together and Mama was on the outside with her back to them.

A scrap of a verse he'd learned in Sunday school when he was younger than Lashanda came to him. Something about a person standing apart.

> *But Love and I had the wit to win:*
> *We drew a circle that took him in.*

That image suddenly troubled him so much that he slipped out of the room as silently as he'd come. What did circles of love have to do with this anyhow? They loved Mama and Mama surely loved them.

Look at the way she took care of them, the way she cooked good food and kept the house so neat and clean. Not like Willie's mom, who half the time sent him out for pizza or KFC and didn't seem to care if dishes piled up in the kitchen or if people dropped clothes and toys and schoolbooks wherever they finished with them so that she couldn't have vacuumed or dusted even if she'd wanted to.

Unbidden though came memories of the way Mrs. Parrish could throw back her head and roar with laughter over something Willie said, how Sister Jordan would reach out and suddenly crush her grandsons with big warm hugs for no reason at all, how old Brother Frank and Sister Hathy Smith still held hands when they walked across the churchyard despite their canes.

When did Mama quit laughing and hugging them? he wondered. Or holding Dad's hand? Because she did use to.

Didn't she?

He shook his head angrily, hating himself for these disloyal thoughts. Mama loves us, he told himself firmly, and we love her. She's just busy doing good things for people. She sees that Sister Jordan's grass is cut, sees that nobody at Balm of Gilead goes hungry, and even though she doesn't like dealing with white people, she doesn't let that stop her from driving over to Dobbs whenever some of the congregation need help signing up for benefits.

She makes sure all the shut-ins get their Meals on Wheels and that they have a ride to the clinic for their checkups.

And look how she loaned her car to Miss Rosa yesterday so Miss Rosa wouldn't lose her job when her car broke down Friday.

Mama's prayer partner was a cheerful person. Rough as she had it, she could always find things to laugh about when she came to visit, outrageous things white people did where she worked, things that made Mama shake her head and cluck her tongue.

Dad thought Miss Rosa was using her, but Mama just shrugged at that. "We're here to *be* used, Ralph," she reproached him. "How can I see your church members struggling and *not* try to help?"

As Stan entered the kitchen, he could see his mother and Rosa Edwards through the open door that led out to a screened porch. The two women sat facing each other across a small wicker table. The Bible was open between them, but their hands were clasped, their heads were close together and Miss Rosa was speaking with low urgency.

Both of Clara Freeman's children knew better than to interrupt a parent's conversation, so Stan went to the doorway and waited quietly until one of the women should notice him.

Miss Rosa saw him first and sat back abruptly, as if startled.

"What is it, Stanley?" his mother asked sharply.

"May I have a glass of lemonade, Mama?"

"Yes, but be sure and wipe up the counter if you spill any. I don't want ants in my kitchen again. Lemonade for you, Rosa?"

"I shouldn't. In fact, I probably ought to go." The other woman shifted in her chair, but didn't get up. "I've hindered you too long already."

"You never hinder me," said his mother with a smile

for her friend. She closed her Bible and put it aside. "Stanley?"

Without spilling a drop, he brought a brimming glass out to the porch and set it down in front of Miss Rosa.

"Thank you, honey," she said.

"You're welcome."

As he returned to the kitchen, he heard Miss Rosa say, "You're raising you a fine young man, Sister Clara."

"We're real proud of him," his mother said.

As she always said.

Sunday dinner long over, the kitchen restored to order, the chattering nieces and nephews and their noisy children now departed, Cyl DeGraffenried's grandmother rested drowsily in her old oak rocking chair. The chair had a split willow seat that her own mother had woven half a century earlier and Mrs. Mitchiner kept it protected with a dark blue cushion. No one else ever sat there and the child who dared put his skinny little bottom on that cushion without being invited risked getting that bottom smacked.

Mrs. Mitchiner gave a dainty yawn and settled herself more comfortably in the chair.

Cyl nudged a small footstool closer and said, "Wouldn't you rest better if you went and lay down for a while?"

"I'm not ready to take to my bed in the daytime yet," Mrs. Mitchiner said tartly.

As Cyl had known she would. Unless she were sick, her grandmother never lay down until bedtime. If the sun was up, so was she. Her only concession to sloth was to lean back and let her spine actually rest against the cushion.

"See you next Sunday, then," said Cyl as she bent to kiss that cool pale cheek. "Call me if you need anything."

The older woman caught her hand. "Everything all right with you, child?"

"Sure," Cyl said cautiously. "Why?"

"I don't know. This last month, there's something different. I look at you in church. One minute you be sad, next minute you be lit up all happy."

Green eyes looked deep into Cyl's brown.

"Oh, baby, you finally loving somebody?"

"You, Grandma," she parried lightly. "Just you."

"I may be old, but I'm not feeble-minded," said Mrs. Mitchiner. "Just tell me this. Is he a good Christian man?"

"He tries to be," Cyl whispered.

Satisfied, Mrs. Mitchiner leaned back in her chair. "That's all God asks, baby. That's all He asks."

At the Orchid Motel, Marie O'Day was showing her newest employee the ropes. Mrs. O'Day didn't speak much Spanish and if Consuela Flores understood much English, it wasn't obvious. Nevertheless, they managed to communicate well enough that when they came to the last room at the back of the motel and found a Do Not Disturb sign on the door, Consuela pointed to the work sheet and made an inquisitive sound.

"Good!" said Mrs. O'Day with an encouraging nod and exaggerated pantomime. "*Este* guest no check out at noon, and it's past three o'clock." She tapped her watch and held up three fingers. "*Qué más*? What you do now?"

Confidently, the apprentice maid stepped up to the door and rapped smartly. "Housekeeping!" she called in a lilting accent.

Sunlight played on the low bushes that separated walkway from parking lot and a welcome breeze ruffled the younger woman's long black hair as she listened for an answer. When no one responded, she used the master key to open the door, again announcing herself.

Inside, the drapes were tightly drawn, but enough sunlight spilled through the doorway to show that the king-sized bed had not been slept in. The near side pillow had been pulled up against the headboard and the coverlet was rumpled where someone had sat. Otherwise the bed was still made. An overnight case sat open on the luggage bench under the window and a cosmetic bag lay on the dresser next to a bottle of wine and two plastic goblets, familiar signs that this guest was still in residence even though the room had been booked for only one night.

Consuela Flores looked to the motel owner for instructions.

"Start with the bathroom," Marie O'Day said briskly, pulling the curtains to let more light into the room, "then we'll—"

"*¡Cojones de Jesús!*" Consuela shrieked. Crossing herself furiously, she recoiled from her path to the bathroom and slammed into Mrs. O'Day.

A torrent of Spanish poured from the terrified maid and she clung to her employer, who looked over her shoulder to the figure that sprawled on the floor between the bed and the far wall.

It was a slender blonde white woman.

She was naked except for black bra, a black lace garter belt and stockings. One sheer black stocking was on her leg. The other was knotted tightly around her neck.

CHAPTER 4

A faint rise in the barometer may be noticed before the sharp fall follows. Wisps of thin, cirrus cloud float for 200 miles around the storm center.

Election day was still two months away and I had no Republican opposition. Nevertheless, I continued to hit as many churches as I could every Sunday I was free. Today was homecoming at Bethel Baptist, the church that my mother and Aunt Zell had grown up in, not to mention my sister-in-law Minnie and Dwight Bryant as well. I hadn't planned to go, but then I hadn't planned to be free either.

Instead, I dragged my aching bones out of bed early and with my own two hands and a recipe off the Internet, I made a perfect pan of lemon bars for the picnic dinner that followed the preaching services. I also contributed a deep-dish chicken pie prepared from ingredients I'd bought Friday evening when I still thought Kidd was coming.

"Didn't know you could cook anything besides popcorn," said Dwight, helping himself to a spoonful.

"And you still won't know till you actually taste it," teased Seth, who was right in behind him.

Seth's five brothers up from me and likes to pretend I can't tie my own shoelaces yet.

"Y'all leave Deborah alone," said Dwight's mother. "I know for a fact that Sue started teaching her how to cook before she was five."

I love Miss Emily. Whenever she's putting Dwight in his place, she always looks like a militant Chihuahua up against a Saint Bernard. I'm told that Dwight and his sister Nancy Faye take after their dad, a big slow-moving deliberate man who was killed in a farming accident when his four children were quite young. The other two look like Miss Emily, who is small and wiry and has bright orange hair.

She's the enormously popular principal of Zachary Taylor High School and drives an elderly TR that she turns over to the vocational kids for a new paint job every spring. They think she's pretty cool because no matter how outrageous the color or detailing, as long as it isn't pornographic, she drives the results for a year. Currently, the car's a midnight blue with a ferocious cougar splayed across the hood. Last year it was turquoise with flamingoes and palm trees and the year before that, a neon purple with red and yellow racing stripes.

I took a serving of her pear salad. With so many newcomers from all over the whole country, Colleton County church picnics are no longer just home-fried chicken and ham biscuits. These days the chicken's likely to come out of a fast-food bucket that'll be plonked down alongside a bowl of guacamole or eggplant parmigiana. But Miss Emily's pear salad is unpretentious comfort food from my childhood: canned pear halves on buttercrunch lettuce with a blob of mayonnaise in the center and a healthy sprinkle of shredded American cheese. Even though I wind up scraping off most of the cheese and mayonnaise, I still put it on my plate every time it's offered.

Miss Emily was pleased and took me around and introduced me to all the new people who've moved in since I last visited. In between, we paused to hug and reminisce with old-timers who remembered my mother and still knew Aunt Zell. If everybody was speaking gospel truth that Sunday, I could count on a hundred votes right here.

I was surprised Aunt Zell and Uncle Ash hadn't come, but Minnie said they were spending the weekend with cousins down on Harkers Island. "I think she was hoping they might could have a hurricane party."

People were talking about beach erosion from the storm surges Edouard had kicked up as it passed by our coast, but a hundred and fifty miles inland, the weather here was downright pleasant—low 80s, low humidity, nice breeze. In fact, the day was much too beautiful to stay inside and after all the preaching and handshaking (*and* a helping of fresh banana pudding from the dessert table), I wanted some physical activity. My whole body was still a little sore and achy from last night and I knew just what it needed.

"Anybody for a swim off my new pier?" I asked

when I'd worked my way back around to Seth and Minnie.

"You know, that sounds like fun," said Minnie with a pleased smile. "I haven't been in the water this whole summer."

Miss Emily begged off, but Dwight thought he'd swing by for a while if he could find an old bathing suit at her house.

"Come on anyhow," said Seth. "I got an extra, don't I, hon?"

"If you don't, Robert or Andrew will," said Minnie.

I packed up the remains of my chicken pie and lemon bars and stopped at a store on the way home for a bag of ice, some soft drinks, salsa and several bags of tortilla chips in case this turned into another picnic.

The long pond that my house overlooks is actually more like a small lake that covers about five acres. Years ago, Daddy scooped out a marshy bottom when the little twins thought they wanted to raise catfish as a 4-H project. When they got over that enthusiasm, the original pond was drained, bulldozers and back- hoes enlarged it to its present size and it was restocked with bass, bream and crappies.

The land Daddy deeded me takes in only the eastern third of the pond. The rest is part Haywood's and part Seth's, but of course, the whole family use it as freely as if all the land still had Daddy's name on the deed.

When I drove into the yard, I saw two fishermen in our old rowboat at the far end of the water. One was definitely Daddy—I could see his truck parked under a willow tree down there. I assumed the other was one of my brothers or nephews. At a distance, they tend to look a lot alike. I waved before taking my bags into the kitchen and putting the ice in a cooler.

By the time I got the food stowed and then called around to the rest of my brothers who still live out this way, cars and trucks were pulling into my yard—Minnie and Seth, Andrew and April, Andrew's A.K. and Herman's Reese. Haywood and Isabel were in Atlantic City this weekend, Robert and Doris weren't home, and Zach's wife and daughter Emma were visiting Barbara's sick grandmother in Wilson, but Zach said he'd come as soon as he could find out what she'd done with his swimsuit. (Half of my brothers still act like they're guests in their own homes and don't have a clue as to where anything's kept even though their wives have been putting stuff back in the exact same places since the day they were carried across the thresholds.)

Long as I had the phone in my hand, I called Will and Amy over in Dobbs and they said they'd try to make it before dark.

That's when I finally noticed the message light blinking on my answering machine. Two messages actually. The first was from Kidd and came about five minutes after I left for church this morning: "I know I said I couldn't come, but this is dumb when we both have Labor Day off tomorrow. Call me back and say if it's okay if I scoot on up there this afternoon. I really miss you, Ms. Judge."

All *right!* His words zinged a warm flush through my body. "Take *that*, Amber, baby!" I thought gleefully.

A moment later, my emotions took a plunge into ice water as I listened to Kidd's second message.

"I guess you must be at church or something. Oh, God, Deb'rah, I sure do hate to have to say this. Some asshole hunter took a potshot at Griggs this morning. Got him in the shoulder. He's going to be okay and the shooter's in jail, but they just called me out to cover for him. Damn, damn, *damn!*"

My sentiments exactly as I angrily reset the message tape.

"Hey, it's not Kidd's fault that his colleague got shot," reasoned the preacher who lives in the back of my head.

The pragmatist who shares head space agreed. "The situation's exactly what it was before you heard his message. Nothing's changed."

"Except that he lifted me up and then let me drop again," I sulked out loud.

"So? Since when do you take all your emotional cues from somebody else?" they both asked.

Point taken, I decided, and I made myself breathe deeply till I calmed back down. Just in time, too, since my yard seemed to be filling up with large animals. Through the window, I saw Zach's teenage son Lee, Andrew's Ruth and Seth's Jessica arrive on horseback, escorted by Blue and Ladybelle, the farm's boss dogs, and a couple of Robert's redbones.

How Herman's Annie Sue over in Dobbs had heard so quickly, I didn't know, unless she was already on the farm, but here she was, getting out of her car with her friend Cindy McGee, and both wore bathing suits under their T-shirts.

Since it was just family and nobody I needed to impress, I changed into a faded old black bathing suit and topped it with a "big-and-tall" white cotton dress shirt that Haywood outgrew this spring. It's loose and airy on me, perfect for keeping the sun off my bare arms.

Until I had this house of my own, I hadn't quite realized how much I loved giving parties and having people come.

Seth, who was helping me carry lawn chairs from the garage, smiled when I said that. "Must be the Mama Sue in you."

"That woman sure did know how to throw a party," agreed Dwight, putting a couple of chairs under each arm. He'd arrived in a bathing suit and T-shirt as faded as mine, his Sunday-go-to-meeting clothes on a hanger in his truck.

Mother's parties and her hospitality were legendary. I had neither the space nor the help that she'd had, but I liked the thought that I might be carrying on her tradition.

The kids were jumping in and out and Minnie was bobbing around on a big fat inner tube when I got down to the pier. We'd had so much rain this month that the pond's surface was almost even with the pier and I jumped right in. The water's deep enough there to take a running dive off the end, but I've resisted all entreaties for a real diving board.

"Only if you all agree to wear helmets," I tell my nieces and nephews, having seen too many head injuries for one lifetime.

(They tell *me* I'm starting to sound like their parents.)

"Here comes Granddaddy!" called A.K. "Race y'all to him."

The water boiled with furiously stroking arms and

kicking legs as they churned off toward the approaching rowboat. I let them go. After yesterday's ball game, the muscles in my arms were too sore for competition.

Daddy and whoever was with him had either fished all they wanted or else the bass weren't biting because my swimming area was too far away to seriously disturb the fish at that end.

Dwight pulled himself onto the pier and he slicked his wet hair back with both hands, then shaded his eyes against the sun. A pleased smile lit his face as the boat came closer. "Well, looky who's here."

It was Terry Wilson, a special agent with the State Bureau of Investigation and one of my favorite ex-boyfriends. Terry came between a law professor at Carolina and the current assistant secretary of a state department in Raleigh that shall remain nameless. I came between wives number two and three. Daddy's crazy about Terry and had sort of hoped I might be number three, the good woman that would settle Terry down and give him a stable home life.

As if.

Kidd included, Terry's more fun than any man I've ever known, but I wasn't reared to take a backseat to any body or any thing and he'd made it clear up front that his boy Stanton came first and the job came second. Since he was working undercover narcotics back then, I soon saw the futility of trying to take our relationship beyond the fun and games. Wife number three didn't last long enough to wreck our friendship and Terry still makes me laugh with the best war stories of any of my law enforcement friends.

I had a matching grin on my face as he rowed the old boat toward my pier.

Terry and Dwight and some of my brothers played baseball in the same high school division. They still go hunting together and he has standing fishing privileges in all the ponds on the farm.

Just as Terry threw the rope to Annie Sue to tie up, Dwight's pager went off.

He muttered a mild oath and looked around as if to see a phone magically appear.

Actually, one did. Annie Sue's friend Cindy had her cell phone tucked into the pocket of her T-shirt that was hanging on one of the pier posts. "Help yourself," she told him.

I pulled myself out of the water and listened un-abashedly.

Dwight still had his watch on and I saw him check the time. "Around three-thirty, you say? And you got there ten minutes ago? Good. Secure the scene and call for the van and backups. I'll be there"—again he checked his watch—"in, say, twenty-five minutes, thirty at the most."

He replaced Cindy's phone and said, "Okay if I change clothes up at the house, Deb'rah?"

"Of course," I said.

Terry shipped the oars and stepped up onto the pier. "You got to leave the minute I get here?"

"Yeah," said Dwight. "Somebody went and got her-self killed at the Orchid Motel over in Dobbs."

CHAPTER | 5

**What caused the mighty elemental distur-
bance, the possibilities of its recurrence
and the danger which constantly hangs
over other cities are given in detail.**

A murder out on the bypass? Naturally enough, we
assumed that whoever got killed at the Orchid Motel
was a tourist who probably brought her own problems
as well as her killer from somewhere outside the
county. Nothing to concern us beyond the usual curiosity. Our momentary gloom was perfunctory and
more because it was dragging Dwight away than because of an anonymous death.

"Too bad," we said. We clicked our tongues and
shook our heads, then went back to the pleasures of a
lazy warm Sunday. As the sun began to set in a blaze of
gold and purple, the menfolks dressed the bucket of
fish Daddy and Terry had caught while Minnie and I
made cornbread and salad.

My back porch is fully screened and plenty big for a large round table and lots of chairs. The table was one I'd found in Robert's barn and works just fine when I hide the water stains and scratches with a red-checkered tablecloth. The chairs at the moment are cheap white plastic deck chairs and I only have four. Even with the four from my dining area inside, we were going to have to fill in with those folding aluminum lawn chairs that are always just a little too low for any eating table.

Some of the kids don't like fish, so I fetched a couple of twenties and was going to send Reese and A.K. out for pizzas, but they'd already conferred with the rest of their cousins and decided that the seven of them would stop somewhere on their way into Garner for a movie they all wanted to see at the new multiplex.

"But we sure do 'preciate your generosity," said Reese, plucking the bills from my hand with a big grin.

Zach had to leave, too. "Barbara'll be home soon and we're supposed to go over and take supper with her sister." He cast a regretful eye at Minnie's corn-bread.

With the dogs milling around his feet, Daddy sat on the porch steps downwind from Terry and lit a cigarette while they watched Andrew and Seth fuss with getting the charcoal hot enough. The grill was one that Haywood and Isabel gave me when they bought a new gas model last month and this was the first time I'd had it out.

April murmured sounds of dismay as she rummaged in my sparsely filled kitchen drawers and cabinets for plates, glasses and flatware. All she could find were three or four mismatched plates and mugs, four glasses and some odds and ends of tableware—discards Aunt Zell had given me till I could get around to buying new.

"Over there," I said, gesturing toward the cupboards Will had built into the wall behind my dining table.

Mother was townbred and of the generation of young women that picked out table patterns by the time they were sixteen and registered them at Belk's or Ivey's. Her family was solidly middle-class, with a wide circle of equally well-to-do friends who gave her at least a dozen bridal showers, which means that she brought a ton of china, silver, and crystal to the farm when she married Daddy, a dirt farmer who'd never before even held a silver spoon, much less eaten from one.

She had willed it all to me, her only daughter, and when I moved into my new house, Daddy boxed it up and brought it over on the back of his old Chevy pickup. Full-service china for sixteen with meat platters, lidded bowls, and tureens. Silver for twenty. Enough crystal wine goblets to drink France under the table. It took up every inch of Will's cabinets.

"You can't serve cornbread and pond fish on Royal Doulton," April protested. "Do you know how much it would cost to replace one of those plates?"

"Why?" I asked with a perfectly straight face. "Did you plan on breaking some?"

"Deborah!" It was the same voice she would have used on one of her sixth-grade students.

"Look," I said. "This stuff hasn't been used since Mother died and Christmas was about the only time she ever used it herself. It's either that or paper plates and plastic forks and I hate plastic forks."

We compromised. Paper plates, plastic cups, sterling silver.

"We should have given you a proper housewarming," Minnie said and April nodded.

I laughed. "Come on, you two! Cotton Grove may *think* it's ready for the twenty-first century, but housewarmings for single people?"

"We could have started a trend," Minnie said regretfully.

"Never mind," April told her. "It'll make Christmas easy on all of us for the next few years. You've always been hard to shop for, Deborah. Now we can give you house stuff. Stainless flatware and water glasses." An impish grin spread over her freckled face. "And cute little napkin rings and salt-and-pepper shakers shaped like kittycats."

"Don't forget Tupperware," said Minnie.

"Teflon!"

"Aprons!"

"Oven mitts that look like vegetables!"

Laughing, they stepped onto the porch to set the table and Seth called through the screen. "I guess we're skipping church tonight?"

Minnie gave him an inquiring look. "Unless *you* want to go?"

"Well, I believe I'd rather sit right here and give thanks for this fish and this company," Seth said happily.

In the end, nine of us sat down to supper because Amy and Will arrived just as the first, smaller fish were coming off the grill.

"Sorry we couldn't get here in time to help," Amy said.

"That's okay," Terry said magnanimously, as if catching half the fish cleared him of further obligations. "You and Will can wash dishes."

Will took one look at the disposable plates and cups and said, "Done!"

Amy took one look at the silver and said, "You don't put *this* in your dishwasher, do you?"

"Why not?" I asked.

April had just taken a bite of crusty cornbread, but she rolled her eyes at Minnie, who laughed and passed me the salad.

Pond fish, bass excluded, are too small to split or scale if you're going to grill them, and they're full of bones. They're also wonderfully succulent and these were cooked to perfection.

"Fresher'n this and they'd still be swimming," said Daddy, as he expertly laid open a little sunperch and deboned it.

The first few minutes were devoted to food talk, then Seth mentioned Dwight and how he had to leave for a homicide at the Orchid Motel.

Amy looked up in interest. "Any of y'all know Lynn Bullock? We heard that's who it was. One of the EMS drivers told somebody in ER that she was choked to death. They say Tom and Marie O'Day found her stark naked with just a black stocking tied around her neck. Stiff as a board, too."

Amy works on the administrative side at the hospital and hears every rumor that floats through the medical complex.

"Lynn Bullock?" I asked, removing a small bone from my mouth. "Not married to Jason Bullock?"

Amy nodded. "She's one of our LPNs."

I put down my fork. "That can't be right. I was sitting next to him at the ball game last night when she called him from a motel in Yanceyville."

"How'd he know?" asked Will.

"I assume he knows his own wife's voice."

"No, I mean how did he know she was calling from Yanceyville?"

"Because she and her sister had gone antiquing up there."

There was a slightly cynical smile on Will's lips, a smile just like the one on Terry's. Though butter wouldn't melt in either mouth these days, both men know a thing or two about creative cheating. There's a reason they've both been married three times.

Seth and Andrew merely looked interested. Seth because he's never looked at another woman since Minnie, Andrew because, even though he messed up two marriages before April came into his life, infidelity was never the problem.

"Bullock," said Daddy. "Didn't one of Vara Seymour's girls marry a Bullock?"

"I believe her mother's name *is* Vara," said Amy. "But I was thinking Lynn's maiden name was Benton."

"Likely was," Daddy said, helping himself to another fish. "Vara, she sort of got around a bit."

"Who's Vara Seymour?" Minnie asked.

"Charlie Seymour's girl. Little Creek Township. He used to do some work for me. She were a pretty little thing, Vara were, but her mammy died when she was just starting to ramble and Charlie didn't know nothing about raising a girl."

From his tone of voice, I could guess what work

Lynn Bullock's grandfather had done for him. He's out of the business now, of course, but Daddy was once one of the biggest bootleggers on the East Coast and he'd financed a string of illegal moonshine stills all over this part of the country before Mother reformed him.

"I don't know what kind of a woman her mother was," said Amy, "but Lynn herself was bright as sunshine."

"Won't never nothing wrong with Charlie Seymour's brains," Daddy said mildly.

"Excellent LPN," Amy said. "She was really good with scared pre-op patients. One of those people who never saw a stranger. She'd start in talking to them like she'd known them all her life. Didn't mind getting her hands dirty either. A lot of doctors are going to miss her."

"But not all?" I asked, picking up on something in her tone.

"Well-l-l."

"What?"

Amy shrugged. "I don't think we have to worry about Dr. Potts crying at her funeral. Lynn got her husband to represent Felicia Potts for their divorce."

"What's so bad about that?" asked Terry as he took another piece of cornbread.

"Ask Deborah."

The Potts divorce took place in May so it was still quite clear in my mind. It was the first case Jason Bullock had argued before me. Might have been his first case in association with Avery and Avery, for all I knew. Equitable division of marital property in a bitterly contentious divorce.

Felicia and Jeremy Potts had met and married at
Carolina. Felicia soon dropped out and went to work
full-time in order to help Jeremy get his undergradu-
ate degree, then to send him to med school. Nine
years later, having completed medical school and his
residency at Dobbs Memorial, and having passed all
his boards, he was poised to join a lucrative private
practice there in Dobbs. At that point, Dr. Jeremy
Potts suddenly decided Felicia hadn't "grown" as a
doctor's wife and he had filed for divorce.

They had been formally separated for over a year
when the case came to me for final disposition. There
wasn't much marital property beyond the furniture in
their rental apartment and two five-year-old cars, and
Dr. Potts generously offered her all the furniture and a
ten-thousand-dollar settlement. He also offered to pay
college tuition if Felicia now wished to go back for a
degree.

Jason Bullock, who had only recently taken on Mrs.
Potts's case, asked me to consider Dr. Potts's own de-
grees as marital property.

"You think you can split up a medical license like a
set of dining room chairs?" sneered the good doctor.

His attorney asked to speak to his client in private.
When they came back to the bargaining table, the attorney announced that Dr. Potts was also willing to
pay reasonable room and board while Felicia was in
college, a term not to exceed three years.

Jason Bullock smiled, then produced pay stubs and
cancelled checks to prove that Felicia had indeed financed most of Jeremy Potts's medical education.

Although our State Supreme Court has ruled that
professional licenses aren't marital property, it has

ruled that "any direct or indirect contribution made by one spouse to help educate or develop the career potential of the other spouse" could be taken into consideration when granting alimony. Bullock's argument and those cancelled checks convinced me that Potts would still be slogging through medical school without his wife's help and I granted Mrs. Potts so much alimony that my clerk's jaw dropped. I even provided for an annual accounting of his income with an accountant of her choice if she decided later to come back for a bigger bite sometime in the future.

Potts's attorney gave immediate notice of appeal.

"You're free to take it to Raleigh," I had told him, feeling pretty sure that my ruling was solidly grounded in the law. "In the meantime, her alimony payments start now."

Most of this occurred in open court and the results were public record so it wasn't a betrayal of anyone's confidence to tell about the case over fish and cornbread.

"But why would Potts be angry at Lynn Bullock," I asked, "when it was Jason Bullock that handled the wife's divorce?"

Again, Amy knew the details. "Felicia Potts studied accounting before she quit school and when they came to Dobbs, she got a job in Ralph McGee's office till he died."

(The late Ralph McGee, father of Annie Sue's friend Cindy, had been a CPA over in Dobbs.)

"That's how she met Lynn. Ralph did the Bullocks' taxes."

"And that affected the Potts divorce?" asked Minnie.

"Absolutely! Felicia was going to accept the good doctor's first offer," said Amy, "and Lynn heard him bragging about it at the hospital. I told y'all Lynn Bullock was one smart cookie? When Jason was in law school, she used to read some of his casebooks and one of those cases covered a similar situation. Felicia didn't have any money to hire a good lawyer and it'd never dawned on her that a degree could be like marital property, but once Lynn talked Jason into taking the case on a contingency basis, Felicia went back and pulled every tax record and every receipt from their whole marriage."

Daddy nodded. "Sounds like something a granddaughter of Charlie Seymour's would think of."

"Lynn Bullock?" Will cocked his head at his wife. "Long blonde hair? Built like a brick outhouse? Wasn't she the gal we saw Reid with at the North Raleigh Hilton last Christmas?"

"Well, I wasn't going to speak ill of the dead," Amy said, "but yes, she *did* play around on the side a little."

Again Daddy nodded. "Just like her mama."

CHAPTER 6

Such a night of horror as the unfortunate
inhabitants were compelled to pass has
fallen to the lot of few since the records of
history were first opened.

September 1—cont'd.
—Edouard 37.5 N by 70 W. Winds 85 knots & dropping
fast as it heads to N. Atlantic. No longer a threat to any-
body.
—Hurr. Dolly pounded Mexico. At least 2 people dead.
—Fran 23.9 N by ?? W. Winds steady at 75 kts.
—Gustave—

Stan threw down his pencil, unable to concentrate.

Upon returning from evening worship, he had come
straight to his room and turned on his radio to the
weather station, but he'd been too distracted to copy
off all the numbers accurately, much less put them in
coherent order. There were floods in Sudan, mon-
soons in Pakistan, earthquakes in Ecuador and maybe

he'd use them in his report and maybe he wouldn't, but right now, all he could think about was the storm raging behind the closed door of his parents' bedroom.

A quiet storm. No flying shoes or hair irons crashing into lamps. No shrieked accusations or thundering counterblasts. Even with his own door cracked, he could barely hear his mother's low voice, quick and tight and cold with a towering anger usually reserved for racist whites who threatened the dignity of her world.

Normally when she raged, his father's voice would be heard rumbling beneath hers, soothing, reassuring, reasoning. Tonight, he seemed to speak only when she paused after a torrent of questions, and even then, his words were short and fell away to a silence quickly filled with more of her anger.

Bewildered, Stan remembered how the evening had started normally enough. After a heavy Sunday dinner, supper was always sandwiches and milk. Then Mama and Lashanda would neaten up the kitchen while he and Dad went on ahead in the van to get things set up.

Ever since Balm of Gilead burned to the ground back in July, services had been held in an old-fashioned canvas gospel tent with folding chairs. In just the few short months Dad'd been here, the congregation had grown to over a hundred and it looked as if they could begin breaking ground for a new sanctuary next month. Meantime, everybody was sort of enjoying the outdoor preaching. There were inconveniences, of course. No Sunday school rooms, no choir stalls, no screens, no air-conditioning, not even overhead fans, only the hand-held, cardboard-and-stick fans with a picture of Jesus knocking at the door on one side and an ad for a funeral home on the other.

But tent revivals were a tradition that had almost fallen out of use and the older folks beamed when they sang,

Gimme that ol' time religion, that ol' time religion,
Gimme that ol' time religion—It's good enough for me.

That evening, he'd helped Dad set up the simple sound system, then he'd taken rubber gloves and a bucket of soapy water out to the two portable toilets that stood modestly on opposite sides of a large holly tree at the back of the lot and wiped down the seats and floors so everything would be neat and fresh.

When he came back to the tent, Sister Helen Garrett and her daughter Crystal were there, arranging a large bouquet of deep blue hydrangeas in front of the pulpit, the only piece of church furniture to survive the fire. At least Crystal was at work on the flowers, trying to keep the heavy flower heads from tipping over. Her mother was at the pulpit in deep talk with his father.

"Hey, Stan," Crystal said shyly. They were in the same class, but different homerooms at school, and he'd only started to know her a little when Sister Garrett joined their church last month. "Could I borrow your bucket to get some water for these?"

"I'll get that for you," he said, glad for a chance to be alone with her a few minutes before his friends arrived and started clowning around, teasing them. He'd always had friends who were girls, but never a real girlfriend. Not that Crystal *was*, he thought confusedly as he fetched the water and poured it into the vase. But if he did have a girlfriend, Crystal Garrett sure would be *fine*. That smile. Those eyes. Smart, too. Her science project was on the life cycle of the black-and-yellow argiope.

Only thing wrong was her mother, who embarrassed both of them the way she put herself forward at calls for rededication, clinging to Dad as she sobbed out her sins in his ear. Now that his own body was so aware of girls—and not just Crystal—it had only recently dawned on him precisely why Sister Garrett and one or two other of the church women took any opportunity to convert Dad's "right hand of fellowship" into a warm hug. He hated the way those women pulled at him and touched him and brushed up against him like they wanted more from him than what a pastor was supposed to give.

Crystal wasn't responsible for her mother any more than he was for Dad, who couldn't help reaching out and touching whoever he was speaking to at the moment. Like now, when one of the deacons approached and he drew Brother Lorton into the conversation with a handclasp and an arm around the older man's shoulder.

Predictably, once the conversation quit being one-on-one, Sister Garrett turned her attention back to the flowers and, to his dismay, to him. "You're looking more like your daddy every day, Stanley. No wonder my little Crystal's so sweet on you."

Crystal looked as if she wanted to go crawl under the pulpit and Stan escaped by suddenly remembering that he was supposed to distribute hymn books and fans along the chairs. More church folks arrived and he answered politely as they greeted him. He hadn't noticed Mama and Lashanda's arrival until his little sister edged up to him while he was plugging in the lights and whispered, "Mama's real mad."

Guilt had instantly seized him. A dozen possible transgressions immediately tumbled through his mind.

"What's she mad about?" he asked cautiously.

The seven-year-old shook her head, her brown eyes wide with unhappiness. "I don't know. I think she found something in Daddy's desk."

Four things were off-limits without permission: the refrigerator except for milk or carrots, the cookie jar, their parents' bedroom unless Mama or Dad was there, and Dad's desk in the living room.

Doors and drawers were left unlocked. It was enough for Mama to say "Thou shalt not" to ensure that neither he nor Lashanda would open any of them unbidden. They knew that Dad kept his pastoral records in the desk and often sat there to counsel troubled church members.

Maybe that's what Mama's found, he thought. Maybe there were some notes about a member of the congregation who'd done something so steeped in sin that the church needed to cast them out.

There was that time in Warrenton when she'd urged Dad to take such a step, but Dad had brought the sinner back to Christ. "And if Jesus can forgive him, Clara, who are we to cast stones and cast him out?"

But he couldn't say all this to his sister. She was still too little to understand.

"Don't worry. Dad'll take care of it," he reassured her, and she'd skipped away to join her friends.

Crystal had saved a place for him among their friends near the back but he kept a wary eye on his mother's profile. She sat in her accustomed seat, the very last chair on the front row.

As the pastor's wife, Mama knew all eyes were always upon her and her children and she preached to them constantly.

"It's up to us to set good examples," she said. "Think before you act. Weigh your words before you speak. The Bible tells us that the ungodly are like the chaff which the wind driveth away. The Devil is a mighty wind, children, and he'll blow your bad words and bad deeds to where they'll do the most hurt to your father if you're not mindful of who you are."

So Mama had sat in her usual seat and kept her face turned to Dad's with her usual expression of solemn attention. But when preaching was over and everything was stowed in the back of the van, Mama gave her keys to Miss Rosa, who was still without her own transportation to work, and she and Lashanda rode home with them. That's when he realized that Dad was the focus of her anger.

As his parents approached the van, he heard Dad say, "What were you doing in my desk, Clara?"

"I was looking a rubber band for my prayer cards." Her words lashed out like a switch off a peach tree. "Instead, I found—"

She hushed when she realized that the van windows were open and that Stan and Lashanda were sitting wide-eyed.

There was utter silence as they drove home and he and Lashanda had immediately gone to their rooms without being told. It was like seeing bolts of lightning flash across a dark sky and scurrying for cover before the storm broke.

He couldn't imagine what Mama had found to set her off like that.

"Rubbers!" Clara Freeman's face contorted with distaste as she voiced a word that raised images of filth and abomination in her mind. "An open pack. I had my tubes tied after Lashanda, so why do you have rubbers in your desk, Ralph? What whore you lying down on? I'm your true wife, the mother of your children. I yoked my life to yours, walked beside you in righteousness, sacrificed myself to your calling."

"Clara, don't," Ralph said. It was worse than he'd imagined when he let himself imagine.

"Haven't I done what I promised the day you asked me to marry you?" she raged in quiet fury. "Haven't I been an upright and faithful helpmeet? Taught our children to walk in the ways of our Lord Jesus Christ and respect your position?"

Battered by her anger, knowing he was responsible for her scalding humiliation, he mumured, "You have."

"What more could a man of God require of a wife?"

He shook his head, suddenly deeply tired. "Sometimes, even a man of God just wants to be treated like a man, Clara."

She drew herself up icily at this allusion to sex. "I've done my duty to you in this bed."

"Your duty," he repeated, feeling numb.

"So now it's my fault? Because I won't be your whore in bed, you've gone to a whore's bed?"

"I never meant to hurt you," he said quietly.

"Hurt *me*? It's not just me that's hurt, it's you, it's the children, but most of all, it's God. When people see a preacher turn to adultery and fornication, they laugh with the Devil and it's God who's hurt."

"Clara—"

"Did you think you could keep her a secret? When all the eyes of the church are on its shepherd? I'm your true wife, Ralph, and I call you back to the paths of righteousness. Like Sarah to Abraham. In the name of God, I tell you to cast out your concubine like Abraham cast out Hagar."

"Oh, Clara—"

The sound of her name upon his lips fed her scornful rage like kerosene on an open flame. Suddenly, she whipped her dress over her head and flung it to the floor. Her slip followed, then her bra and panties. For the first time in years, she stood naked before him.

Naked with all the lamps on.

"Is this what you want from me, Ralph?" She cocked her hip at him and did an awkward parody of a bump and grind. "Is this what it takes to redeem your soul?"

A sheen of perspiration covered her face and light gleamed on her full breasts and smooth belly. She was thirty-six years old and had borne two children, yet her body seemed as slim and firm as on their wedding night, the night he realized he had made a huge error that could never be rectified, when he understood that he'd mistaken her passion for God as a passion for him.

She had given him her virginity as a burnt sacrifice to God, not as a celebration of God's greatest gift between man and woman.

Now she slowly turned around, displaying herself

openly, front and back. "Am I not comely in your sight?"

As she came back full circle, she saw the pity in his eyes and abruptly tried to cover herself with her arms and hands.

"Oh, God!" she moaned and dropped to her knees at the foot of their bed, clasped her hands and began to pray, wordlessly, silently, with tears streaming from her closed eyes.

Ralph opened their closet, took her white cotton robe from the door hook, and gently draped it around her shoulders. Without opening her eyes, she pulled the fabric across her naked breasts and continued to pray.

As Ralph stepped out into the hall and closed the door behind him, he saw that Stan's door was slightly ajar and he pushed it open.

The boy looked at him. "Is something wrong, Dad?"

He had never lied to his children. "Yes, but it's between your mother and me and we'll work it out. Try not to let it trouble you any more than you can help, okay?"

Wanting to be convinced, his son nodded.

"Don't stay up too late," said Ralph.

"I won't. 'Night, Dad."

"'Night, Daddy," echoed Lashanda's little voice from next door.

His daughter was already in bed with the lights out, but enough spilled in from the hall when Ralph opened her door to see that she was still wide awake. He adjusted the fan in her window and asked if she was cool enough.

"Is Mama still mad?" the little girl whispered.

"She'll be fine in the morning," Ralph said, knowing that Clara would be in firm control of her emotions by breakfast time. Even if she were still angry with him, she would try not to let the children see it.

He kissed Lashanda goodnight and went down the hall to the living room. The telephone sat on the desk that had betrayed him and for a moment he was tempted to call.

But what he had to say to Cyl couldn't be said on a telephone, he decided. He pulled his keys from his pocket and walked out into the night.

The Bullocks lived in a small rental house at the edge of Cotton Grove.

There was only a single streetlight at the far end of the quiet block, but a light was on by the front door, and as soon as Dwight pulled up to the curb in his Colleton County cruiser, he saw a man come to the front window and peer out at him.

The door was opened before Dwight could cross the yard.

"What's happened?" he called from the porch. "Is it my wife? Is she all right?"

"Evening, Mr. Bullock," Dwight said.

Even though both had played softball together the night before and eaten pizza at the same table afterwards, Dwight was now in full official mode and Jason Bullock stopped dead on the porch steps as he registered the deputy sheriff's formality.

"Was she in a wreck? She always drives too fast. Oh Jesus, I'll *kill* her if she's gone and hurt herself!"

The contradiction of words would have been funny

if Dwight didn't know what was going on in the man's head, that he was bracing himself to hear what a rumpled officer of the law had come to tell him at ten o'clock at night.

"I'm sorry," Dwight said. "There's no easy way to say this—"

"She's *dead?*"

All the air seemed to go out of Jason Bullock and Dwight put out his hand to steady him.

"Oh, Jesus," he moaned. "I told her and told her, but she wouldn't slow down. I swore I was going to buy a clunker that wouldn't go over forty miles an hour and she just laughed. Oh, Jesus. What happened?"

"Where was your wife this weekend, Mr. Bullock?"

"She drove up toward Virginia—there were some antique stores near Danville. Look, are you absolutely sure? I mean, her sister was with her. Maybe they made a mistake?"

Dwight shook his head. "No mistake."

"She called me just before our game. She said she'd bought me a surprise. She said she loved—"

His face crumpled and he sank down on the wooden steps that led onto the porch.

Awkwardly, Dwight patted his shoulder.

"Sorry," Bullock said. He fumbled at his pockets, stood up and went into the house.

Dwight followed through the open door and into the kitchen where Bullock pulled a handful of paper towels from the dispenser by the sink and blew his nose.

The kitchen table was set for two with a bowl of slightly wilted salad in the center. A couple of steaks had thawed on the drainboard and runnels of blood had dried on the white porcelain.

"What about Lurleen?" asked Bullock when he had his emotions in check. "Her sister. Is she okay?"

There was no way to mask the truth. Quietly but succinctly, Dwight explained that his wife had never left Colleton County. That she hadn't died in a car crash, that she'd been murdered in the Orchid Motel out on the Dobbs bypass.

"What?" Bullock was looking like someone had sucker-punched him. *"Why?"*

As neutrally as possible, Dwight described how his wife had been found—the wine glasses, the black lingerie, her partial nudity, how the door showed no sign of being forced.

Bullock listened numbly, his jaws clenching tighter and tighter with each new humiliating detail, till faint patches of white appeared along his chinline.

"I'm sorry," Dwight said again.

"Where is she?" he asked abruptly. "What do I need to do?"

"We sent her body to Chapel Hill for the autopsy," said Dwight, "but they're fast. If you have a funeral director call, they'll probably be finished within twenty-four hours."

He pulled a plastic bag from his pocket. Inside was a slim ballpoint pen. Sterling silver and expensive. Not an advertising gimme, although it looked elusively familiar to him for some reason. They had found it under Lynn Bullock's body though he didn't tell her husband this.

"Is it hers?" Dwight asked.

Jason Bullock took the bag and looked closely at the sleek design. "If it is, I never saw it before."

He looked at Dwight bleakly. "But I guess there's a lot I didn't see, huh?"

CHAPTER 7

These storms, which are common to the southern and southeastern coasts of the United States, invariably originate in "the doldrums," or that region in the ocean where calms abound.

Monday morning—Labor Day—and I was surfing channels, trying to find more details about Lynn Bullock's death while waiting for the coffee to perk. All I was getting were the bare facts voiced over uninformative shots of the Orchid Motel draped in yellow police tape from yesterday afternoon, although a helicopter view from above showed me that the motel was closer to the ball field than I'd realized. All the time Jason was talking to his wife, thinking she was a hundred miles away, she was right there less than half a mile from us.

The TV reporters didn't seem to know as much as Amy had. I felt sorry for Tom and Marie O'Day, who bought the motel six years ago and have worked hard to make it succeed. This wasn't the kind of publicity they needed. Tom appeared on camera long enough to say they had nothing to say, and viewers got to see a draped gurney being wheeled from a ground-floor room at the back of the building.

The radio was even less informative.

What I really needed was a newspaper.

When I lived with Aunt Zell and Uncle Ash, the *News and Observer* was lying on the breakfast table every morning when I came down. The *Dobbs Ledger*, too, if it were Monday, Wednesday or Friday. (With all the new people and new businesses coming into the county, the *Ledger* has also grown. Back in June, Linsey Thomas started publishing it three times a week instead of twice.)

Now that I have my own house, I also have my own subscriptions and both papers are delivered right on schedule.

The difference is that Aunt Zell has merely to open her front door and pick up the papers from her welcome mat. My mail and paper boxes are just over half a mile away from my front door, down a long and winding driveway, and this presents me with something of a moral problem.

Only a total sloth would use a car for a one-mile round trip, but I'm a pitiful jogger and walking takes too long. So I half-walk, half-run and when I get back, all hot and sweaty, with *Ledger* newsprint smearing my hands because Linsey won't change the presses over to smudgeless ink, I might as well jump in the pond and swim till I'm out of breath before I shower and shampoo my hair.

Keep in mind that I am *not* a morning person. Before eight o'clock, all I really want is a reviving cup of coffee and a quiet moment to read the paper. Being forced to work out first thing is not my idea of how to start the day, although I have to admit that the new regime's done wonders for my muscle tone.

Some days, if I'm pressed for time, I do drive down, but I always feel so guilty that it takes the edge off the morning. You think it's silly to equate walking with righteousness and driving with sin?

Me, too.

But my Southern Baptist upbringing is such that nine mornings out of ten will find me puffing down the long drive. Which is why I was standing in a clump of yellow coreopsis at the edge of the road reading about Lynn Bullock's death when Dwight drove by around nine that morning and stopped to ask if I wanted a lift back to the house.

"Sure," I said, opening the passenger door of his cruiser. (Riding in someone else's car doesn't seem to bother my conscience.)

I was wearing sneakers, a sports bra and denim shorts with no underpants because I planned to swim as soon as I got back and half the time I don't bother with a suit.

"So who killed the Bullock woman?" I asked. By then I'd scanned both papers and seen little new since both went to press before the victim's identity had been announced.

"Now you know I can't talk to you about this."

"Sure you can," I wheedled. "I don't gossip—"

He snorted at that.

"I've never repeated anything you ever asked me to keep to myself," I said indignantly, "and you know it."

"True."

"And homicide cases are never heard in district court, so it's not as if you're tainting a trial judge."

"Also true." He gently braked and I felt the under-side of the car scrape dirt as we eased over a patch where the tire ruts were deeper than the middle.

"Well, then?"

"You need to get Robert or Haywood to take a trac-tor blade to this drive again," he said.

"Dwight!"

"Okay, okay. Not that there's much to tell yet. Bul-lock gave me his sister-in-law's number up in Rox-boro, but she never answered her phone till this morning. Said she hadn't talked to Mrs. Bullock since Tuesday night. Didn't know anything about a trip to Danville this weekend. She herself spent the weekend with a sailor in Norfolk."

Dwight pulled into my yard and cut the engine when I invited him in for coffee. I'd turned on the cof-feemaker just as I left for the papers and it was fresh and hot. I poured us each a mugful, toasted a couple of English muffins, added figs from Daddy's bush and the last of the blueberries from Minnie and Seth's and then carried the full tray out to the porch table. Dwight had switched on the paddle fan overhead and it stirred the air enough to make the difference be-tween pleasant and uncomfortable.

Hurricane Edouard was still dumping water on New England, but here in Colleton County the skies were bright blue with a few puffy clouds scattered overhead.

We buttered our muffins and topped each bite with the fresh fruits.

"Anybody see anything at the motel?"

"We don't have statements from all the help yet, but so far, nothing. That unit was the end one on the back side of the building and the trees and bushes back there are so thick that Sherman's army could've camped for a week without anybody seeing 'em. The people in the nearby units checked out yesterday before the body was found and we're trying to contact all of them. The O'Days run a clean business, but if someone wants to pay by cash, they don't ask to see ID and that's what happened with the guy in the next unit. Connecticut license plate. We're just hoping he didn't lie about his plate number."

"How's Jason really taking it?" I asked, popping a plump and juicy blueberry against the roof of my mouth.

"'Bout like you'd expect. Doesn't know whether to be mad or sad. She was his wife, but she was screwing around on him."

"Any chance he could've done it?"

We're both cynical enough to put spouses at the top of any list of suspects.

Dwight shrugged. "Always a chance. He seemed pretty shook when I told him last night. He was at the ball field when you and I got there and his car was in front of us all the way back to Cotton Grove. Of course, he could have got home, found something that told him where she really was, and roared back to Dobbs by ten-thirty. We'll have to wait for the ME's report. One good thing though—they ought to be able to pinpoint the time of death pretty close."

"Oh?"

"Yeah. The motel's shorthanded right now since school started, so Tom and Marie were both working the weekend. He had a bowl of peanuts on the registration counter and she ate a few when she checked in. Tom thinks that was around four-thirty, quarter to five."

He didn't have to draw me a picture. Depending on how far along digestion was, the ME should be able to bracket the time of death rather narrowly.

"Tom had never met her, didn't know who she was and he didn't think twice when she paid cash in advance and gave him a phony name. Benton."

"Her maiden name," I said.

"Now how you know that?"

"She was an LPN at the hospital. Amy and Will got here after you left yesterday."

That was enough. He knows Amy, knows where she works, knows how she picks up information and stores it like a squirrel laying up pecans for winter.

"Amy says she played around."

"Any names?"

"Not recent ones," I hedged as I nibbled more blueberries.

"Her sister swears she'd hung up her spurs and was walking the straight and narrow these days," said Dwight, "but you wouldn't know it from the way that room looked."

He took another swallow of coffee. "Anyhow, Tom O'Day says she knew exactly where she wanted to be. Asked for a ground-floor room in back, said she liked it quiet and didn't want stairs. It was the last non-smoking room left on that side. According to the switchboard records, she made only one outgoing call on her room phone after she checked in. Around five."

"To her husband. I was sitting in front of Jason when he talked to her."

"And the switchboard says she received an incoming call about ten minutes after that, someone who asked if Lynn Benton had checked in yet."

"Male?"

"The operator thinks so, but can't swear to it. She also says somebody called around three o'clock asking the same thing and that it could've been the same person."

"Impatient lover just waiting to find out what room she was in before rushing over?"

"Sounds like it, since he knew what name she was using."

"Nobody saw her at the drink machine? Filling her ice bucket? Letting strange men into her room?"

"If they did, they're not saying."

"I guess you're pretty sure it *was* a man?"

"Dressed like that? Or rather, undressed like that? And she was pretty well-built. Taller than you. Probably stronger, too. Nurses do a lot of lifting and pulling. It would've taken somebody just as strong."

"He could've caught her off-guard," I said, picturing the scene. "He could've been undressing her, took off one of her stockings. Maybe trailed it along her neck."

My mind flinched from the rest of the scenario. Lynn Bullock had thought he was making love to her. Instead—

Across the table from me, Dwight pulled a fig apart to reveal the soft fleshy interior and I wondered what he was thinking as he ate it. Ever look closely at a fig? It's male on the outside, explicitly female on the inside. Erotic as hell, but I doubt if Dwight notices.

"We bagged her hands," he said, "but if the killer came up from behind with that stocking and threw her down face-first, she may not've had time to do more than claw at the thing that was choking her. If that's the case, we'll only find her own DNA under her nails."

"Poor Jason Bullock." I sighed and got up to fetch the coffeepot for refills.

When I came back from the kitchen, Dwight was holding a couple of plastic evidence bags in such a way that his big hands concealed the contents.

"What's that?" I asked.

"These really do stay confidential," he warned me. "Ever see this before?"

Inside the first plastic bag was the top part of a gold-toned tie tack. Less than half an inch wide, it was shaped like a tiny American flag.

"Ambrose Daughtridge wears tie tacks," I said. "And so does Millard King, but I never paid much attention to them."

"What about this, then? We found it under the victim's body. For some reason, it makes me think of you. Why?"

It was a silver ballpoint pen.

"Because I had one just like it on my desk at the law firm," I said promptly. "You must have seen it there. John Claude gave them as Christmas presents three or four years ago."

Mine was in a pencil cup by the telephone in my bedroom and I brought it out to show Dwight. "I don't carry it in my purse because I'm afraid I'll put it down somewhere and walk off without it."

Dwight smiled as he compared the two. He knows my theory that there are probably only about fourteen ballpoint pens in Colleton County and everybody keeps picking them up at one business counter and putting them down at another counter somewhere down the road.

These pens were sterling silver—John Claude doesn't give cheap presents—and were distinctively chased with tendrils of ivy that twined along the length of the barrel.

"Any fingerprints?"

"Just smudges. Who else got one besides you?"

"I'm not sure. You'll have to ask John Claude." I didn't like where this was going. "Reid got one and Sherry Cobb."

Sherry is the firm's small, bossy office manager and Reid, of course, is the current generation's Stephenson.

Lees and Stephensons have been law partners since John Claude's father (a cousin from my Lee side) began the firm with Reid's grandfather (my great-grandfather) back in the early twenties. Southerners sometimes exaggerate the ties of kinship, yet family loyalties do exist and most of us will always give a cousin the benefit of doubt, even a first cousin once removed, as Reid was. His sexual development may have stopped when he was in junior high, but that doesn't make him a killer.

I didn't care if Will and Amy *had* once seen them together, there was no way Reid could be involved in

Lynn Bullock's death, and I wasn't going to offer him up as a candidate to Dwight.

"I think John Claude bought them at a jewelry store at Crabtree Valley," I said. "Dozens of them are probably floating around the Triangle."

"We'll check," Dwight said mildly. "Long as Reid has his, no problem, right?"

I keep forgetting how well he knows me.

CHAPTER 8

> Ordinarily, men and women have enough
> to do in attending to their own affairs, ex-
> pecting others, of course, to do the same,
> and consequently they pay small attention
> to what is going on around them.

After Dwight left, I finished reading the paper. Polls showed Jesse Helms with his usual slim lead over Harvey Gantt in the senate race—what else was new?—and NASCAR champion Richard Petty was several points ahead of Elaine Marshall for Secretary of State, though that gap had closed a little since the last poll. Nothing to get our hopes up about though.

The *Ledger*'s front-page story carried a studio portrait of Lynn Bullock. Even in black and white, her makeup looked overdone and her long blonde hair was definitely overteased. More Hollywood than Colleton County.

("Meow," scolded my internal preacher.)

Sheriff Bo Poole reported that his department was following up several important leads and he appealed to the public to come forward if anyone had seen Mrs. Bullock or anything suspicious at the Orchid Motel between five p.m. and midnight on Saturday.

In true *Ledger* fashion, the story ended by listing Lynn Bullock's survivors: her husband, Jason Bullock "of the home"; her sister, Lurleen Adams of Roxboro; her mother, Vara Fernandez of Fuquay-Varina; and her father, Cody Benton of Jacksonville, Florida.

I was mildly bemused to see Dr. Jeremy Potts pictured at the bottom of the same page, along with another white-jacketed doctor. They flanked a piece of diagnostic equipment that was evidently state-of-the-art. The story was about the machine, not the doctors, so I turned to the sports pages to check out the softball pictures.

Linsey's new photographer might have been slow with names, but he was expert with the camera. White or black, all our faces were crisp and clear. I never push, but I do make sure I'm always on the front row. Every bit of public notice, no matter how tiny, has to help subliminally at the polling booth.

Putting the plates and mugs Dwight and I had used in the dishwasher, I wiped down the countertops, then swept the kitchen and porch floor clean of crumbs and sand from last night. It'll be next spring before my centipede grass is thick enough to make a difference with tracked-in sand. In the meantime, no matter how many doormats I scatter around, I live with the sound of grit underfoot. It's almost as bad as a beach house.

At Aunt Zell's, I kept my two rooms picked up and I chipped in on her twice-a-month cleaning woman, but that was about the extent of my domestic labors. Now I'm doing it all myself and part of me is amused to watch the surfacing of a heretofore latent pleasure in housework, while the other part is horrified to see myself slipping into such a stereotypical gender role.

"Long as you don't start crocheting potholders or make people take off their shoes before they come in," soothes my mental pragmatist.

By noon I had changed the linens on my bed and had just thrown sheets and towels in the washer when my friend Dixie called from High Point. She said she'd get me a visitor's badge if I wanted to come over at the end of next month's wholesale furniture market to pick up a few floor samples at dirt-cheap prices.

"Should I keep my eye out for anything in particular?" she offered.

Standing in the middle of my house and looking around at all the bare spots that surrounded a handful of shabby family castoffs, I hardly knew where to start. "A couch?" I said. "And maybe a really great coffee table? That's all I can afford right now."

We talked about styles and colors and whether her love life was as stalled as mine seemed to be at the moment.

Yet, as if to give lie to all my grumbling, the phone rang the instant I hung up and it was Kidd, who did a lot of grumbling on his own about having to work time and a half to compensate for his wounded colleague when he'd rather be upstate with me.

"Tell me what you're wearing," he said.

"Right this minute?"

"Right this minute."

I slipped off my sneakers and curled up on the old

overstuffed couch handed down from April's aunt. "My purple knit bra and a pair of cutoffs."

"That's all?"

"Hey, I'm decent."

"Not for long."

I smiled. "Why not?"

"Because I'm sliding the straps down off your shoulders and over your arms."

"You are?"

"I am."

"And I'm letting you?"

"You have no choice," he teased. "The straps are keeping your arms pinned to your side while I pull the bra down around your waist and kiss you all over."

"Um-m-m," I murmured, settling deeper into the cushions. "Feels wonderful." It seemed so long since we'd touched that I closed my eyes and drifted as his voice added detail upon erotic detail.

"I'm not as helpless as you think, though," I warned him softly. "You've pinned my arms, but my hands are free and I'm unbuttoning your shirt . . . running my hands across your chest." My voice slowed and deepened. "I'm touching your nipples very lightly, barely brushing them with my fingertips."

My own breasts began to tingle as he told me where his lips were and described what his hands were doing. I could almost feel the roughness of his stubbled cheek, his face pressed hotly against me.

"Now I've unbuttoned the top of your shorts," he said huskily. "My fingers are on the zipper . . . Slowly, very slowly I—"

The screen door slammed and a male voice said, "Hey, Deb'rah? You home or not?"

I was so into the spell Kidd was weaving that for one confused moment, I felt as if I ought to clutch a cushion to my chest to hide my nakedness. Between telephone and washer, I hadn't heard Reid Stephenson's car drive up.

"Oops!" he said as he poked his head through the door and saw me. "Sorry. Didn't realize you were on the phone. I'll wait. Go ahead and finish."

As if.

Mood shattered, I told Kidd I'd call him later.

" 'Fraid I won't be here," he said with a long regretful sigh. "Roy and me, we're patrolling the water tonight. Lot of drunk boat drivers'll be out. But, Deb'rah?"

"Yes?"

"Remind me to punch your cousin in the nose the next time I come up, hear?"

"Hey, you didn't have to get off the phone on my account," said Reid.

"Yes, I did," I said grumpily. "What're you doing out this way anyhow?"

Dressed in dark red shirt, white sneakers, no socks, Reid just stood there happily jingling his keys in the pocket of his khaki shorts. Not only is he cute as a cocker spaniel puppy with his big hazel eyes and his curly brown hair, he has a puppy's sunny good nature and isn't easily insulted, which is probably why he's so successful with women. Takes more than a whack with a newspaper to discourage him when there's a tasty treat in sight.

"I brought you a housewarming present."

He beckoned me out to the porch. There on the

table was a long flat box wrapped in brown paper, tied with a gingham ribbon and topped with a spray of what looked like dried grasses.

"What's that stuff?" I asked.

He grinned. "Hayseeds, of course."

It's been a running joke with some of my town friends that my move to the country was the first step toward turning into a country bumpkin, that I'd soon be coming to court with a stem of broomstraw dangling from the corner of my mouth.

Inside the box were two smaller packages. The first was a yellow-backed booklet covered with dense black typescript that advertised things like blackstrap molasses, copper arthritis bracelets and diuretics—an old-fashioned farmer's almanac.

"You need to know what signs to plant your crops under," Reid said.

I had to smile because Daddy and Maidie still consult this same almanac before they plant—a waxing moon for leafy vegetables, dark of the moon for roots, zodiac signs for everything else.

The other package contained a rather handsome walnut board, inset with three brassbound dials. The top one was a thermometer (86°), the middle was a barometer (29.6"), and the bottom recorded the humidity (58%)—actually a pleasant day for the first week in September.

"How about beside your bathroom door?" Reid suggested as I looked around for a place to hang it. "You can see what the weather's like as soon as you get up every morning."

As if I couldn't just look out the window. But he was

so pleased with himself and his gift that I held my tongue.

We carried it into my bedroom and he was right, as he usually is about spatial concepts. It was a perfect fit. One of the reasons Reid's such a good trial lawyer is that he notices details. So far as I knew, he'd only been in this room once since I moved in, when he brought out a small bookcase from my old office a few weeks back, yet he remembered the narrow wall between my closet and bathroom doors.

"Get me a screwdriver and I'll go ahead and put it up for you," Reid said.

I fetched one from the garage and we hung it in less than five minutes.

"Dwight see you this morning?" I asked as we walked back through the kitchen and I transferred my wet laundry to the dryer.

"About that pen he found under Lynn Bullock?"

"He told you that?"

"Come on, Deborah. I'm an attorney, remember? I don't answer any questions from a deputy sheriff without a good reason. Soon as you told him they were Christmas presents from John Claude, you knew he'd come asking to see mine."

"And you showed it to him?" I asked casually.

"Not yet. It's back at the office. He's going to come by tomorrow when I'm there. But I got to tell you, it pisses the hell out of me that he won't take my word for it. Has anybody *ever* seen me raise a hand to a woman? Ask Dotty. Bad as we used to fight, the only thing I ever slammed was the door."

"But you did have an affair with Lynn Bullock," I said.

He shook his head. "Nope. We went out twice last winter, I slept with her once and that was it."

Genuinely curious, I asked, "What's your definition of an affair?"

"More than a quickie and two suppers, that's for sure," he said virtuously. "Not to speak ill of the dead, but she turned out not to be my type."

"Oh?" I hadn't realized there *were* such creatures.

"Lynn Bullock was a sexy woman and she really liked to—" He hesitated. John Claude's lectured him so many times about using the F-word in front of women that it's starting to sink in. "—to do it. The thing is, she was just a little too trashy for me."

He spoke with such a straight face that I couldn't control my laughter.

"After Mabel, the motorcycle mama?" I hooted. "Or little Cass with the big—"

"You don't have to call the roll," Reid said, offended. "Look, you know Dolly Parton's famous remark?"

" 'It takes a lot of money to look this trashy'?"

"Right. But Dolly goes for that look deliberately. It's her stage persona. Earthy. Playful. Lynn Bullock wore the same big hair, flashy clothes, and gaudy costume jewelry, only she was dead serious. She thought it made her look upper-class—I swear to God, she must've spent her formative years studying *Dynasty* as if it were a documentary on tasteful dressing."

"I never knew you were such a snob," I said.

"I'm not! Lynn was though. The first and only time I f—I mean, laid her, she spent the rest of the evening classifying half the people in Dobbs—this person was, quote, 'society.' That one was 'low-class.' I thought at first she was being funny but, no, ma'am! She was dead serious and she had the pecking order in this county down pat. I told her that if she wanted to see a real pecking order, she ought to come with me to the Rittner-Kazlov Foundation reception at the North Raleigh Hilton and watch artists and musicians put each other in their places. Mother wanted me to go represent her and I'd had just enough bourbon to think it might be amusing to watch Lynn watch them."

(Between them, Brix Jr. and Jane Ashley Stephenson have sat on half the non-profit boards in the Triangle.)

"I'm guessing all the women showed up in earnest black gowns and ceramic necklaces?"

"I believe there were two maroon velvets and an authentic batik with strings of cowrie shells."

"And Lynn Bullock wore—?"

"A bright green satin cocktail suit with the skirt up to here, hair out to there, gold shoes, gold purse, chunky gold earrings and gold glitter in her hair. She said she hoped the glitter wasn't too much, but after all it was Christmas."

"Oh, Lord." I've always disapproved of extramarital sex, but I could almost find it in my heart to feel sorry for someone that tone-deaf about clothes. "How on earth did she get out of the house dressed like that without her husband noticing?"

"He was in Charlotte that weekend."

"So how did the artsy crowd react?"

" 'Bout like you'd expect. Polite for the most part, but there was a lot of eye-rolling and the older women became very, very kind to me, almost motherly. They did everything except cut up my carrot sticks for me."

"Poor you."

"The worst was running into Amy and Will as we were leaving. Amy took one look at Lynn and then sort of glazed over. But what really iced the cake was the way Lynn thought those women were jealous of her style. She didn't have a clue." Reid shook his head.

"The weird thing was that even though she was out with *me*, cheating on *him*, she kept talking about how great it was going to be when her husband joined Portland and Avery's firm—how much money Jason was going to make and how they were looking forward to the day when they could afford to sponsor civic events because money's the way you get your nose under society's tent."

"She got that right, didn't she?" I said cynically.

More than forty years ago, my daddy's own acquisition of respectability was based on the illegal production and distribution of moonshine. Mother's people were higher up the social scale and after they fell in love and married, she made him quit bootlegging. Without that early seed money though—the whiskey money that bought good bottom land, decent equipment, and a fair amount of respect—he probably would have stayed too dirt poor to court her in the first place.

"Who would kill her, Reid?"

"Hell, I don't know. Usually you'd say the husband, but Bullock was on the ball field, right? Millard King, too."

"She slept with Millard King? When?"

He shrugged. "Before me, after me, during me—I don't keep tabs. I just remember hearing their names linked." He paused a moment. "Come to think of it though, not recently. I heard he's hoping to marry the daughter of one of our Justices."

He shook his head again. "I really don't know who was sleeping with her. Not me, though."

"Any problem walking away?" I asked, trying to get a feel for the murdered woman.

"Not for me," he said, with that male arrogance that always annoys the hell out of me. Then he gave a sheepish grin. "Cost me a bundle to get the smell of dog dirt out of my car, though. She dumped a whole pile of it all over the front seat."

CHAPTER 9

Dejection and despondency succeeded
fright.

*September 3—Edouard—no longer anything but an ex-
tratropical storm at 6 a.m.—just south of Nova Scotia—
winds only 55 kts. Large swells, minor beach erosion, some
coastal flooding from NC–Maine. Some damage to
small boats at Martha's Vineyard & Nantucket. At
least one drowning.
—Fran 24.4°N by 70.1°W—still a Category 1 hurr. &
getting stronger. Will prob. be upgraded to Category 2 by
tonight.
—Gustave's collapsed.
—Hortense*

"Stan? Mama says come to breakfast *now* or we're
gonna be late for school."

Reluctantly, the boy turned off the radio, shelved
the notebook and followed his sister down the hall to

the kitchen. Yesterday's breakfast had been so strained that he'd volunteered to help Dad cut the grass around the church tent without being asked, just to get away from the house. Not that Dad hadn't been quiet and withdrawn himself. But his silences were always more comfortable than Mama's.

To Stan's relief, his mother seemed to be in her normal school morning mode. Wearing a pink-and-green-checked cotton dress, she gave him a good-morning smile as she sliced bananas and peaches over their bowls of cold cereal. His father asked the blessing, then she poured Lashanda's milk and handed the carton on for him to pour his own. Her voice sounded just like always as she passed out lunch money, looked critically at his shirt to see if it was a clean one, and reminded Lashanda that she had piano today, "so don't forget to take your music. I don't want to have to come rushing over to the school this morning, you hear?"

"Yes, Mama." The little girl smiled, too young to worry whether everything really was back to normal. As long as no visible storm clouds hovered over their heads, the semblance was sufficient and she chattered so freely that even Stan felt the tension level go down.

Ralph Freeman finished eating first and went to brush his teeth. When he came back to the kitchen with his backpack hanging from one shoulder, he said, "I have to leave now, Clara, if I want to get to Dobbs on time. You sure you don't want me to drop the children off on my way?"

"You go on ahead," she said, from the kitchen sink. "Rosa gets off at seven and she'll be here in plenty of time. You'll probably pass her on the way."

That's when Stan realized that his mother's car wasn't in the drive. Miss Rosa must've worked the night shift again. As his father bent to kiss them good-bye, he also realized that Mama still had her back to them. Spoons and dishes rattled against each other beneath the running water and she acted too busy to turn around and lift her face for his usual kiss on her cheek. Dad must not have noticed either, because he didn't hesitate, just went on out to the van and drove off.

Rosa Edwards gave a mighty yawn as she drove through morning traffic. Not that she was all that sleepy, merely ready for her own bed after two nights away from it. Sunday night was payback for when Kaneesha covered for her a couple of weeks back, and last night was her own regular night. For people on the housekeeping staff, night duty at the Orchid Motel was mostly a matter of just being there in case a bed suddenly needed changing or fresh towels were required in the middle of the night. Otherwise, there were a couple of lounge chairs in a little room off the main desk where you could put your feet up and doze after you'd tended to all your chores.

The O'Days were good bosses. For white people. They paid better than minimum wage and were real easy to get along with. Of course now, they had their own ideas about how to run a motel and it might not be the way Motel 6 or the Marriott did things, but long as you did your job and did it right, you didn't have to act extra busy when they were around. And they were fair about dividing up the night work. You didn't get hired unless you were willing to take your turn. But you could trade off if you needed to, long as you knew it was your responsibility to see that your hours were covered. That was the one thing they were bad about: show up late or don't show up at all without being covered and, child, the doo-doo don't get no deeper. They didn't want to hear about flat tires, dead batteries or how the babysitter bailed at the last minute. You got one second chance and that was it.

Long line of women be happy to have your job 'stead of picking up sweet potatoes, she told herself. Mexicans, Asians, A-rabs, you name it these days.

Must've been like the United Nations when the police tried to talk to Numi and Tina, who worked the noon to eight shift Saturday and Sunday. Here it was Tuesday morning and that was still all anybody could talk about—that naked body, the black stockings, the fancy wine, the man who'd called twice to see if she was there yet. Not that they were saying much more than that, 'cause nobody'd really noticed the murdered woman when she checked in except for Mr. O'Day.

Sister Clara's car radio was always tuned to a gospel station and Rosa sang along with one of their favorite hymns, but her mind wasn't with the words.

Even though she was on duty Sunday night when yellow tape was being strung all over that end of the place and police cars and ambulances were coming and going, nobody'd interviewed her 'cause they must've been told that she got off work at four on Saturday, before the murdered woman arrived.

None of the others seemed to remember that she came back around five-thirty after doing her weekly shopping because she'd gone and left her Bible in her locker. She hadn't thought anything about it herself till she got there Sunday night and they told her what'd happened in Room 130.

That's when she remembered driving around the back corner of the Orchid Motel in Sister Clara's quiet little car and there was this white man coming out of that very same room. He closed the door and hung the Do Not Disturb sign on the knob and soon as he saw her, he turned away quick-like.

"Jesus, lift me up and lead me on," she sang along with the radio. *"Till I reach your heavenly throne."*

If any policeman had've asked her Sunday night, she might've told about that man right then and there, but all the guests down at that side of the motel, them that didn't just up and check out, had to be moved over to the front side and Mrs. O'Day had kept her hopping till after the police left.

And if anybody'd been with her in the bathroom at two o'clock this morning when she was sitting on the stool reading the *Ledger*, she might've bust out with it then, but they weren't and she didn't. By the time she returned to the lounge, she'd had second and third thoughts about what this secret knowledge could do for her.

"For my sins you did atone," sang the choir.

Yesterday's *Ledger* lay on the car seat beside her, neatly folded so that the man's picture was staring right back at her.

Probably had plenty of money. White men like him usually did. And here she was, needing a new car real bad, what with winter coming on. That old rustbucket of hers stayed in the shop more than it stayed on the road. Wouldn't have to be a fancy car, just something nice and dependable like Sister Clara's.

Sister Clara was always warning her to stay out of white people's business.

Easy enough for her to say, thought Rosa, and her a preacher's wife with a husband to give her everything—nice house, nice car, nice clothes she don't have to go out and work among white folks for. Still, it won't none of her business to bear witness against that man. "Thou shalt not suffer a whore to live." Isn't that what the Bible said? Not up to her to avenge the killing of a white harlot.

Anyhow, she didn't have to decide right now, she told herself. Like Mary, she was going to sit back and ponder all these things in her heart.

"Jesus, lift me up and lead me on."

He couldn't believe his luck. Ever since it happened, he'd checked his rearview mirror for every white Civic that he met, noted every white Civic parked on the streets—who knew Honda had such a big slice of the car market? And didn't they make Civics in any damn color *except* white?

Then suddenly, there it was!

He was waiting at a stop sign when the car sailed by, the gold cross affixed to the license plate, the Jesus bumper stickers with their blood red letters on a white background. The one on the left read, "Jesus loves *YOU!*" The one on the right, "Jesus died for your sins."

Without thinking twice, he immediately switched his blinker from a left-turn arrow to a right-turn. As soon as the westbound lane cleared, he pulled out and headed after the white Civic, his heart pounding. He didn't have a plan. All he'd hoped—a blind illogical hope, he'd begun to think—was that he could somehow find her before she heard about Lynn's death, connected it with him, and went to the sheriff.

Finding her was first. He hadn't really thought about what he'd do after that.

She drove as if she were late, weaving in and out of morning traffic. Fortunately, the heaviest traffic was leaving Cotton Grove, not entering it, and he was able to close the gap between them. Nevertheless, she was four cars ahead of him and he almost lost sight of her when she suddenly whipped into the central turn lane and zipped across in front of an oncoming car with only inches to spare.

He was forced to wait for six cars before he could follow and by then, the white Civic was nowhere to be seen.

Damn, damn, *damn!*

To be this close and then lose her.

He kept to the posted thirty-five miles per hour even though every instinct told him to go even slower so he could look carefully. Unfortunately, this was a residential street in a black neighborhood with black kids collecting on the corner to wait for their school buses. He couldn't afford to drive too slowly or they'd notice him.

Notice and remember.

He told himself that Cotton Grove was a little town and this black neighborhood was proportionately small, too. How long could it take to quarter the whole area?

As it turned out, he didn't have to. Two blocks

down, he spotted the white Civic parked in the driveway of a neat brick house. He carefully noted the house number as he drove by but didn't have time to make out the name on the mailbox, too.

At the next corner, he made a left, then three right turns to bring him back down this street. As he passed the house a second time, he saw two women and two children getting into the car and he immediately pulled in ahead of a green van parked at the curb. He waited there with the motor running till the Civic backed out of the drive. Only the little girl's head turned in his direction when they passed him, and even she didn't seem to notice as he trailed them through town.

First stop was the middle school where she let off the boy, then the elementary school for the little girl. Finally, she stopped in front of a small house at the end of a shabby, unpaved, semi-rural street and the second woman got out. He was too intent on the driver to pay much attention to her passengers. A quick stop at a convenience store, then she drove straight back to the first house.

He was right behind her all the way, and by the time she got out of the car and went into the house with her purchases, he'd begun to formulate his next move. She had to know about the murder by now, yet he hadn't been arrested. Either she hadn't looked at him closely enough to give the police a good description or she hadn't connected him with the murder room. But how could that be unless she was dumber than dirt? She'd driven around the corner of the motel just as he pulled the door closed behind him. He'd certainly registered a black female face and the car's religious symbols as she passed within fifteen feet. It seemed impossible that she wouldn't recognize him the minute she saw him face-to-face again.

He slowed down enough to read the name on the mailbox.

Freeman.

It was a sign.

Take care of that woman and he'd stay a free man.

The blue LCD numbers on her bedside clock marched inexorably toward eight o'clock. Lying there, watching the numbers reconfigure themselves to show every passing moment, Cyl DeGraffenried wondered dully who it was that first realized it would take only seven straight little segments of liquid crystal to display every digit.

She was supposed to be in court at nine, but she couldn't seem to pull herself out of bed. All she wanted to do was lie here and watch those little segments light up or then go dark as the numbers changed.

As an assistant district attorney, she'd seen her share of people with clinical depression and she knew that staying in bed was a classic symptom of withdrawal, but knowing it and being able to resist were two entirely separate things.

Like falling in love with Ralph Freeman. She had known it was stupid and wrong, and she hadn't been able to resist that either.

She considered herself religious, yet she'd never daydreamed of loving a preacher. And certainly not a married preacher.

Two months of unimagined happiness, followed by

these last two nights of misery. Just thinking about Sunday night made her eyes fill up again with tears. Such delight when she'd opened her door to find him standing there.

Such grief when he told her why he'd come.

"You don't love her," she'd said and he didn't deny it.

Instead he took her in his arms as if reaching out for salvation and held her against his heart. "If it were just you and me, I'd walk through the fiery furnace to stay here with you forever. I love you more than I ever dreamed I could love anyone. The smell of you, the softness—" His voice broke with sorrow. "She's the mother of my children, Cyl, and she's done nothing to be humbled like this."

"But she doesn't love you!"

"No," he said bleakly, as his arms fell away from her. "No. But we both love God."

Coming from anyone else, it would have sounded sanctimonious. To Cyl, it sounded hopeless.

"What kind of God would keep the two of you in a loveless marriage?" she had wept. "God *is* love."

"If I left Clara, I'd be turning my back on His love," he said dully. "Breaking all the vows I ever took. I'd be saying that all the things I've preached, all the things I've believed in my whole life, were hypocrisy. I can't do that, Cyl. I can't live without God in my life."

"But God forgives the sinner," Cyl argued, calling upon all the forensic skills that made her such a skilled prosecutor. "He'll forgive us. If you believe in Him, you know that's true."

"Could we forgive ourselves? Could we build a life

on the wreckage of Clara's? Break my children's trust?" He touched her cheek, wet his fingers in her tears and brought his finger to his lips, almost as if it were a communion cup.

"These are my tears which are shed for you," she sobbed, seeing the sacrifice in his eyes. "Take. Drink."

He had crushed her in his arms then with all the intensity of his bitter grief, then, very gently, he had kissed her forehead and walked away.

Leaving her to lie here alone in an empty bed, numbly watching the blue segments come together and fall apart, endlessly marking a time that no longer had meaning.

The partnership of Lee and Stephenson, Attorneys at Law, had begun in an 1867 white clapboard house half a block down from the courthouse back in the 1920s. More than seventy years later, they were still there. When Dwight Bryant stopped in a little after nine, however, he found that this generation's Stephenson hadn't yet arrived.

"Only thing I'm getting's his voice mail," Sherry Cobb apologized. "I'm sure he'll be here directly. Let me fix you some coffee."

Dwight accepted readily. Of all the law firms in town, Lee and Stephenson had the best coffee.

Hearing their voices, John Claude Lee came to the door of his office.

"Got a minute?" asked Dwight.

As soon as he explained what he wanted, John Claude brought out a folder from the file drawer in his desk. As precise and well-ordered as John Claude himself, it was labeled "Christmas Gifts, Office" and after a quick perusal, he was able to give Dwight the brand name and model number of the silver pens, as well as the name of the jewelry store at the Cary Towne Center Mall.

"I bought three," said the white-haired attorney. "One for Reid, one for Deborah, who was still in partnership here that year, and the third for Sherry. Those were my personal gifts to my colleagues. As a gift from the firm the rest of the staff received silver pins shaped like snowflakes with their bonuses."

He returned the folder to its proper place and closed the drawer. "May I assume your interest in my choice of Christmas gifts somehow relates to the death of that unfortunate Bullock's wife?"

"It might, but don't let it get out, okay?"

"My lips are sealed," said John Claude. "Sherry's on the other hand— Would you like for me to ascertain if she still has hers?"

"That would be a big help," Dwight admitted. In addition to having the best coffee, Lee and Stephenson also had the most gossipy office manager. While she was fairly reticent about the firm's business affairs, everything else seemed to be fair game.

"And of course, you'll want to see Reid's." The older man shook his head in weary resignation. His partner's randy nature was a constant trial.

Through the window behind John Claude's head, Dwight spotted Millard King heading down the sidewalk toward the law office next door.

"I'll check back by in a few minutes," he said and hurried out.

Talk about banker's hours, thought Dwight as he cut across the grass on an intercept path. Attorneys don't do too shabby either. Here it was almost nine-thirty, yet Reid wasn't in and King was just arriving.

"Overslept," said Millard King, although he looked alert enough to have been up for hours as Dwight followed him into the two-story white brick building that housed the firm of Daughtridge and Associates. "And I have a ten-fifteen appointment, so I can't give you but just a minute."

"Actually, it may take ten," said Dwight, settling into the comfortable leather chair in front of Millard King's shiny dark desk. "I understand that you were seeing Mrs. Bullock?"

King had worked hard to lose weight this last year, but he was still robustly built and inclined to perspire a little when nervous. He mopped his brow with a snowy white handkerchief, then took off his beautifully tailored gray jacket and hung it on the antique cherry coatstand behind the door before taking a seat behind his executive-sized desk. His shirt was pale blue with white cuffs and collar, his dark blue tie was held in place, not by a tie tack, but by a narrow gold clip. Late twenties, he had the slightly beefy, very blond, all-American good looks of an ex–college halfback who wasn't quite good enough for the pros. Rumors were that he was a fair-to-middling attorney with political ambitions beyond this junior partnership in Ambrose Daughtridge's firm.

King leaned back in his leather armchair, elbows on the armrests, and tented his fingers in front of his chest. "Am I a suspect in her death, Bryant?"

"Should you be?" Dwight asked mildly.

"I'd appreciate it if you wouldn't play games."

The judicious tones would have been more effective without that light sheen of perspiration on his forehead.

"This belong to you, by any chance?" Dwight asked, handing him the bagged flag-shaped tie tack they'd found near Lynn Bullock's body. "I'm told you had one like it."

"Sorry," said King. "I don't recognize it."

"You've heard how she was found?" Dwight asked. "The way she was dressed?"

"And you think *I* was the one going to meet her that night? I was on the ball field," he said indignantly. "You saw me. I hit a double off you, for God's sake!"

"We don't know yet when she was killed," said Dwight. "No one saw her after five or spoke to her after five-ten. Our game didn't start till well after six."

"Well anyhow, I'm covered from around five till our game ended," said King. "I try to run at least five miles a day and on Saturday, I used the school track to run laps from about five-fifteen till shortly before six when I joined the team."

"There's a footpath from the far end of the track, through the trees, out to the bypass. The Orchid Motel is exactly three-tenths of a mile from the track," said Dwight. "We measured."

"But I never left the track," he said tightly. "Dozens of people would have seen me leave or come back. Ask Portland or Avery Brewer."

"Were they out there running with you?"

"Of course not!" King snapped. "I was running alone. I mean, there were other people on the track, but not *with* me."

"Can you give me their names?"

Millard King frowned in concentration, then shook his head. "I didn't know any of them. One man looked a little familiar. He might be a doctor at the hospital, but I couldn't swear to it. Wait a minute! One of the women. She had on red shorts and a white shirt and I think she works in the library. Peggy Some-body."

"Peggy Lasater?"

"Yeah, that sounds right. She'll tell you."

Dwight wrote the name in the little ringbound notebook he carried in his jacket pocket. "What about after the game?"

"Straight home," King said virtuously.

"Which brings me back to my first question. Were you seeing her?"

It was clearly not a question King wanted to answer, but he leaned forward with the earnest air of a man about to put his cards face up on the table.

"Look," he said. "I'm twenty-eight, single, and if a woman comes on to me, looking for a roll in the hay with no commitments, why not?"

"And that's what happened with Lynn Bullock?"

King hesitated. "Is this off the record?"

"I'm not looking to jam you up," said Dwight. "If it's not relevant to our investigation, it stays in the de-partment."

"Okay then. Because, see, I'm about to ask someone to marry me. Someone whose father's in the public eye and who wouldn't take kindly to having his daugh-ter's name linked with a murder investigation. I've been absolutely faithful to her since we first started getting serious this past June and I intend to be faith-

ful from here on out if we marry. I'm not going to
have some little passing affair jump up and bite me in
the ass ten or fifteen years down the road, if you get
my drift."

Dwight nodded, suppressing a grin. Say what you
will about Clinton, he thought to himself, but for
young men with their eyes on future elective office, he
sure had provided a real good object lesson for keeping their peckers in their pants.

"It was at the Bar Association dinner back in April.
She was there with Jason in this tight red dress." He
shook his head reflectively. "If it'd been New York—
hell, if it'd even been Raleigh! But this was Dobbs and
you should've seen all those other women looking at
her sideways and reining their husbands in. Well, I
didn't have any wife and neither did one or two others. You talked to Reid Stephenson yet? Or Brandon
Frazier?"

"Frazier's a new one on me," said Dwight, noting
down the name. "Didn't her husband mind?"

Millard King shrugged. "Some men like it when
their wives make other men hot. Sorta like 'Yeah,
you'd like to get in her panties, but I'm the one she
goes home with.' Jason doesn't miss a trick in the
courtroom but he didn't have a clue about his wife.
Lynn and I got it on a couple of times, but right
around then's when I got serious about the gal I'm
hoping to marry and decided I didn't need that com-
plication."

Something in his virtuous tone made Dwight ask,
"Your idea or Mrs. Bullock's?"

"I guess you could call it a mutual decision," King
admitted.

"In other words, she wanted to break it off more than you did."

"I told you—"

"So if she called you and invited you to join her at the Orchid Motel, you wouldn't have gone?"

"Absolutely not," Millard King said firmly.

At Memorial Hospital in Dobbs, Amy Knott stuck her head in the staff lounge and flourished a manila envelope. "I just wanted to tell everybody that we're collecting to make a donation to pre-op in Lynn Bullock's name."

"I'm sure going to miss her there," said one of the women doctors, handing Amy a ten-dollar bill. "She always went the extra mile. When's the funeral?"

"She's being cremated." Amy held the envelope open as other doctors dug in their pockets. "I understand there'll be a memorial service next month."

The door opened and a white-jacketed doctor came in. He had poured himself a cup of coffee before the unnatural silence finally registered. Spotting Amy's envelope, he said, "Taking up a collection?"

"For Lynn Bullock's memorial," Amy said with a rueful smile. "I don't guess you want to contribute."

"On the contrary." Dr. Jeremy Potts set his coffee down, opened his wallet, and made an elaborate show of pulling out a twenty-dollar bill. "I can't think of anything that would give me more pleasure."

Back at Lee and Stephenson, Dwight was amused to see that Sherry Cobb was using her silver ballpoint pen as she and one of the clerks proofed a long legal document. John Claude smiled benignly from his doorway.

"Reid's in his office," he said, pointing down the wide hallway to what used to be the dining room when this was a private house.

The door was ajar and Dwight rapped on it, then pushed it all the way open. Reid was on the phone and he motioned the big deputy sheriff to come on in as he pushed back his chair so he could open the long center desk drawer. He held the phone in one hand while he rummaged with the other.

"Okay then, Mrs. Cunningham. I'll draft that new codicil and . . . ma'am? . . . No, no, that's quite all right. It'll be ready for your signature tomorrow at ten."

He hung up and continued his search. "That old lady changes her will every time the moon changes. Ah, here it is. *Voila!*"

The morning was so overcast that Reid had his lights turned on and the silver pen gleamed in the lamplight as he fished it out from the back of the drawer and handed it over to Dwight.

Same make, same twining ivy leaves engraved along the length of the barrel.

Reid watched him compare the two pens. "Would you really have thought I killed her if I couldn't put my hands on it?"

Dwight shrugged. "Let's just say it moves you down the list a couple of notches."

"Come on, Dwight. I'm a lover, not a killer. You know that. I've told you—I saw her twice and that was one time too many."

Dwight just nodded and took out his little notebook. "Now as I recall, you got out of somebody's bed and over to the ball field around six. But you left as soon as the game was over. Where'd you go after that?"

114

"I came back here, showered and changed, then drove over to Raleigh. You remember Wilma Cater?"

"Jack Cater's sister?"

"We went to see that new Tom Hanks movie, then stopped by the City Market for a couple of drinks."

"Who's *she* married to?" Dwight asked sardonically.

Reid laughed. "Don't let it get around, but I do go out with *un*married women every once in a while."

At noon, Deputy Mayleen Richards appeared in Dwight's doorway with some papers in hand. "I called the jewelry store and spoke to the manager. The *current* manager."

"Oh?"

"Yes, sir." A tall and solidly built ex-farmgirl, Richards had only recently been pulled off patrol duty. Dwight had decided that her diffidence with him and Sheriff Bo Poole was because she was still ultraconscious of protocol. "There's been a complete change of personnel from when Mr. Lee bought those pens four years ago."

"But?"

"But they do keep pretty good records."

Dwight waved her over to the chair in front of his desk. "So what do these pretty good records show?"

Richards sat down stiffly. "Well, for one thing, the store makes a point of offering exclusive merchandise. They won't carry items you can find at every mall in North Carolina. The pens were made in England and distributed only through an importer in New Jersey. So I went ahead and called them and they confirmed it. The store in Cary Towne Mall was the only outlet between New York and Atlanta that carried the line.

115

There's one in Boston, another in New Orleans." She looked down at her notes. "The rest are Chicago, Scottsdale, Vail, Seattle and L.A. for a total of six hundred pens—a hundred and fifty of them were this design."

"Good work," Dwight said approvingly. "So who owns ours?"

"The jewelry store's old invoices show that they stocked twenty silver pens from that company in four different designs. Five were the 'Windsor Ivy.' They have no documentation as to who bought three of the pens—those have to be Mr. Lee's three—but they do know that two pens were sold at employee discount to the then-manager, who now works in their flagship store in New Orleans."

"Did you call him?" asked Dwight.

"Her," said Richards, allowing herself the smallest of smiles for the first time. "She's not there today, so I left a message that I'd call tomorrow."

"Excellent," said Dwight. "Keep me informed."

"Yes, sir." She handed him some papers. "These are Jamison's interviews with the rest of the motel staff. Nothing useful. And the ME faxed over his preliminary report."

Dwight skimmed through the technical terms that basically said yes, Lynn Bullock had indeed died of strangulation. And based on testimony that she had been seen eating peanuts at approximately 4:45 p.m., it was safe to say that death occurred between the hours of 4:45 and 7:45 p.m.

"Cremated?" gasped Vara Seymour Benton Travers Fernandez. "We ain't never had nobody cremated in

116

our whole family. My daughter ought to've been buried proper and decent, *in* her body, not burnt to ashes."

Jason Bullock looked at his mother-in-law and took a deep breath. "I'm sorry, Vara, but it's what Lynn wanted. We discussed it when I drew up our wills and that's what we both decided to do."

"She never!" Vara said stubbornly. "She ever tell you that, Lurleen?"

"Wills?" said Lynn's half-sister. "She always said she was going to will me her pink ice necklace and earring set. Did she?"

The older woman was skinny as a tobacco stick inside a pair of tight black slacks and a sleeveless top patterned in tiger stripes. Her orangy-blonde hair had been colored and bleached so many times it had thinned until you could see the scalp between the hair follicles. "You mean they's not going to be a church service or nothing?"

"We don't—Lynn didn't—neither of us belong to a church, Vara. It was something we meant to do, but . . ."

Jason Bullock's voice trailed away in regret. A church would have given structure to this hopeless morass he seemed to be floundering through. There would have been churchwomen bringing food and offering comfort, a minister who could have guided him into a traditional ceremony. Instead, he was suddenly thrust into unfamiliar territory and Lynn's only two relatives (if you didn't count her father and a bunch of half-siblings in Florida, and Lynn certainly never had) weren't making it any easier.

He hadn't been able to reach either of them by

phone till early Monday morning. Lurleen immediately drove down from Roxboro, swinging through Fuquay to pick up Vara and bring her over. Now they were back again this afternoon and while there was grief in their eyes, there was also greed in Lurleen's.

He himself was so numb and conflicted at this point that he thought, Well, why not? What else was he going to do with Lynn's things?

"You and Vara can take what you want," he told Lurleen, "but first you've got to tell me. Who was Lynn sleeping with?"

"Just you, honey," she answered guilelessly.

"Ah, cut the crap, Lurleen," he said, suddenly angry. "You know where she died. And how."

She gave a petulant shrug. "She didn't tell me and that's the gawdawful truth. We used to be like this." She held up two crossed fingers. "But ever since y'all got so high and mighty with your fancy jobs and fancy money, she didn't tell me shit. And every time I asked, she'd just smile and say nobody, so she could've been blowing the governor, for all I know."

Tears and mascara cut dusky tracks through Vara's makeup. "Poor little Lynnie. She wanted to be somebody and now she's just ashes. And I didn't even get a chance to kiss her goodbye."

At the stoplight in Mount Olive, as a patrol car pulled even with him in the next lane over, Norwood Love kept his face expressionless, but his eyes went nervously to the pickup's rearview mirror. Everything back there was still secure. There was no way that trooper could see what was beneath the blue plastic tarp covering the truck bed. Besides, even if he *could* see them, there was no law against hauling a load of empty fifty-gallon plastic pickle barrels. For all any-body could say, he was maybe planning to store hog feed in 'em. Or turn 'em on their sides and use 'em for dog kennels. Till they were full of fermenting mash, couldn't nobody prove different.

The light changed to green and the young man pointed his truck back toward Colleton County.

Reid Stephenson's first court appearance of the day was scheduled for two o'clock. As he left the office, he tucked the silver pen securely in the inner breast pocket of his jacket and wondered if Deborah by any chance left her doors unlocked out there on the farm.

Otherwise, he was going to have to figure out an-other excuse to drop by and get her pen back on her bedside table before she missed it.

CHAPTER 10

The air is calm and sultry until a gentle breeze springs from the southeast. This breeze becomes a wind, a gale, and, finally, a tempest.

Despite the long Labor Day weekend in which to get it out of their systems, courthouse regulars were still titillating each other with gossip of Lynn Bullock's death on Tuesday. Who was she having an affair with? Reid? Brandon Frazier? Millard King? Or was it someone yet unnamed? The more malicious tongues favored Millard King, simply because he'd become more priggish now that he was romancing the very proper Justice's debutante daughter. Malice is always entertained when prigs try to squeeze their clay feet into glass slippers.

There were those who thought it was tacky of Lynn Bullock to sleep with so many of her husband's peer group. "Why didn't she keep it at the hospital?" they asked. "All those beds going to waste. Why didn't she crawl into one with a doctor?"

"How you know she didn't?" came the cynical reply. "And come to think of it, wouldn't a doctor know exactly how much pressure it takes to strangle somebody?"

I'd never met the dead woman and I'd had very little to do with her husband so I shouldn't have been drawn into the discussions, yet, given Reid's peripheral involvement, I couldn't help being interested.

Unfortunately, I wasn't hearing much new.

I sat juvenile court that morning—emancipation, termination of parental rights, even a post-termination review, where I learned that two badly neglected twin brothers had been adopted into a loving family. In fact, the new parents were there with the babies, who were clearly thriving. Seeing your decisions vindicated like that is one of the happier aspects of being a judge.

In the afternoon, it was domestic court. There were the usual no-shows and requests for delays, along with a couple of unexpected meetings of minds that only required my signature rather than a formal hearing. By three o'clock, I was down to the final item on the day's docket.

Jason Bullock was scheduled to argue a domestic case in front of me that afteroon—contested divorces seemed to be turning into his specialty, and, under the circumstances, I would have granted a delay. But the plaintiff, one Angela Guthrie, wanted to be done with it and was willing to let Portland Brewer, one of Bullock's senior associates, represent her since she clearly felt any judge in the land would side with her.

Daniel Guthrie was represented by Brandon Frazier, a lean and intense dark-haired man who was also one of the men linked to Lynn Bullock's name. Frazier was about my age, divorced, no children. A lot of women around the courthouse, single *and* married, thought he was sexy-looking with those smoldering, deep-set eyes, but I've never much cared for hairy men. Not that I've ever seen his chest. Looking at the wiry black hair that covers the backs of his hands and wrists gives me a pretty good idea though.

It was the first time I'd seen Frazier since the murder, and if he was walking around with a load of guilt, it wasn't immediately visible. But then it wouldn't be, would it? Every good attorney—and Frazier's pretty good—is an actor and a con man. He has to be able to sell snake oil to a licensed doctor and he does. Why? Because he can make the doctor believe that he himself believes in it—one honorable man to another.

The Guthries were both in their mid-thirties. They had a nine-year-old son and an eleven-year-old daughter. Mr. Guthrie looked somewhat familiar. I seemed to recall him sitting in the witness stand to testify, but for what? Something criminal? My memory was that he'd sat up resolutely and spoken confidently. Today, he had a half-sheepish, half-defiant look about him.

His wife was suing for a divorce from bed and board (which in North Carolina is basically a court-approved legal separation) on the grounds of mental and physical cruelty. She asked for retention of the marital home, custody of the two minor children, child support and post-separation support—what used to be called temporary alimony. Whatever Danny Guthrie had done to her, it was still a burr under her saddle.

According to the papers before me, she'd filed her complaint almost a full month earlier, yet, as she took the stand, I could see that she was madder than hell and it was scorched-earth/sow-the-land-with-salt time.

My friend Portland led her through a recap of marital frictions, all the ordinary, but nonetheless irritating, things that finally drive a spouse to say "Enough!"—his disregard for her plans, his lack of involvement in their children's school activities, his excessive drinking, his erratic work hours.

That was when I realized why Danny Guthrie looked familiar. He was a former K-9 officer with the Fayetteville Police Department, now working dogs for the Drug Enforcement Agency.

"And when did you realize that your differences were completely irreconcilable, Mrs. Guthrie?" asked Portland Avery.

"It was sometime after midnight, the seventh of August. Or more accurately, between the hours of one a.m. and five thirty-eight on the morning of August eighth," Angela Guthrie answered crisply.

"That's remarkably precise," Portland said. "Would you elucidate?"

Green eyes flashing, Mrs. Guthrie described how her husband hadn't come home from work that evening, despite their earlier agreement that they would get up at dawn the next morning and drive to the mountains for a family vacation.

"A vacation that was supposed to give us a chance to relax together and learn to be a family again," said Mrs. Guthrie.

Instead, ol' Danny and Duke didn't come rolling in until well after midnight.

"Duke?" I asked.

"His dog. A Belgian Malinois."

As a judge, I've attended impressive demonstrations of what Malinois can do for law enforcement agencies. They're built like a sturdy, slightly smaller German shepherd and they're intelligent enough to understand several different orders. According to their handlers though, they have to be carefully trained to control a natural tendency toward aggressiveness.

Upset and angry, Mrs. Guthrie had smelled the whiskey on her husband before he got halfway across the kitchen.

"What did you say or do at that point?" asked Portland.

"I was really frosted that he didn't come home in time to help me get ready for the trip and now he was so drunk he wouldn't want to get up till late. *Plus* he'd been too drunk to drive, so we'd have to go get his car before we could get started. I just let him have it with both barrels. I told him exactly what I thought of him and his adolescent behavior," said Mrs. Guthrie, beginning to steam up all over again.

"And what did Mr. Guthrie say or do?"

"He never said a word. Just stood there swaying back and forth till I quit talking. That's when he looked at Duke, pointed at me and said, 'Guard!' and then staggered off to bed."

"What did you do next?"

"*Nothing!*" she howled, rigid with indignation. "Every time I tried to stand up, the damn dog started growling down deep in his chest. I sat there for four hours and thirty-eight minutes till my son came down-stairs and I could send him back up to get Danny."

The bailiff and a couple of attorneys on the side bench were shaking their heads and chuckling.

Okay, I'm not proud of myself. I snickered, too. As a feminist, I was appalled. But as someone who grew up with a houseful of raucous brothers and dogs (dogs that half the time showed more sense than the boys), the thought of that dog and this woman eyeing each other half the night? I'm sorry.

Danny Guthrie misjudged my laugh and when he took the stand to tell his side of the story, he'd re-gained most of the easy confidence I remembered. He seemed to think I was going to be one of the guys, in full sympathy with what he clearly considered a harm-less little prank.

"I'm no alcoholic," he said earnestly. "See, what happened was, our unit had just gotten a commenda-tion for rounding up eight drug runners and we went out to celebrate. Yeah, I probably should've called her, but I didn't realize how late it was. Then I got home and I was really stewed. All of a sudden, that vodka hit me like a ton of bricks and she wouldn't shut up. All I wanted was to get away from her nagging tongue and go to bed. I honestly don't remember telling Duke to guard her. And it's not like he bit her or anything."

"But would he have if she'd tried to leave the room?" I asked.

"Maybe not bite exactly, but he'd of done whatever it took to hold her there."

"You're an officer of the law," I reminded him. "Didn't it occur to you that your wife could have had you arrested for false imprisonment? That you could be sitting in jail for a hundred and twenty days?"

"It was just a *joke!*" he repeated. "She doesn't have a sense of humor."

"Well, in this case, I'm afraid I don't either. What's the difference between what you did and hiring a man with a gun to keep her sitting there? And what happens when it's your weekend to have the children and you've been out celebrating? Would you have Duke guard *them*?"

Apprehensive of where I was going, Guthrie swore he never drank a drop when he was in charge of the children, that he would never put them in jeopardy.

When I asked Mrs. Guthrie the same question, she grudgingly admitted that he was, on the whole, a decent father. Not terribly attentive, but certainly never mean to them or physically abusive in any way.

In the end, despite an eloquent argument from Brandon Frazier, I granted the divorce from bed and board and gave Mrs. Guthrie most of what she was asking for.

The Colleton County Sheriff's Department is located in the courthouse basement and as soon as I'd adjourned court and stashed my robe, I went downstairs to give Dwight the swim trunks he'd left at my house on Sunday and which I'd forgotten to give him when he was out yesterday.

The shifts had just changed and he sat at his desk in short sleeves, his tie loosened and his seersucker jacket hanging on the coatrack. Labor Day might be the official end of white shoes for women, but Dwight never puts away his summer clothes till the weather starts getting serious about colder temperatures.

"Any luck with that man in the room next to Lynn Bullock's?" I asked idly. "The New Jersey license plate?"

We've known each other for so long and he's so used to me asking nosy questions about things that are technically none of my business that half the time he'll just go ahead and answer.

"Connecticut," he said now, distracted by a report he was reading. "No help at all. Turns out the guy's a sales rep for a drug company, on his way home from a sales conference in Florida. Got in around ten, left the next morning before nine. Says he didn't see or hear anything and probably didn't."

Dwight signed the paper he was reading, closed the folder, tossed it into his out-basket, then leaned back in his chair and propped his big feet on the edge of his desk.

"We got the ME's report. He says Lynn Bullock bought the farm sometime between five and eight, although we know she called her husband at five and someone called her at five-ten. That means she was dead before Connecticut ever checked in."

"What about John Claude's pens? Reid and Sherry show you theirs?"

"Yeah. But the store had five to start with. I've got Mayleen Richards working on it."

"There must be hundreds of them like that around," I speculated.

"Not as many as you'd think." He gestured toward the yellow legal pad that lay just beyond his reach. It was covered with doodles and notes that he'd taken when Deputy Richards gave her report. "The national distributor swears that he imported a hundred and fifty and only five of those were sent to this area. 'Course, the way people are moving in from all over, who knows? The whole hundred and fifty could've worked their way back east by now."

I smiled. "Good thing we still had ours."

"Good for Reid, anyhow."

Even though I hadn't *really* been worried about my cousin, I did feel a little relieved that the pen wasn't his.

"You're just going through the motions," I said. "You know you don't think Reid could do a thing like that."

"I quit saying what a person could or couldn't do a long time ago."

Dwight's only a few years older, but sometimes he acts as if those years confer a superior insight into human motivations. He gave a big yawn, stretched full length, then sat upright and opened another folder. "If we don't get a viable suspect in the next twenty-four hours though, I'm going to start looking at all her old boyfriends a little closer. Millard King says he was jogging. Brandon Frazier says he went fishing. Alone. And Reid didn't get to the ball field till after six. Remember?"

I wondered whose reputation would go in the toilet if Reid had to tell what bed he'd been in that afternoon.

Speak of the devil and up he jumps.

Thunder rumbled overhead and rain sprinkled the sidewalks as I hurried toward the parking lot before the heavens opened all the way and drenched my dark red rayon blouse. It isn't that I mind the wet so much, but that particular blouse starts to shrink the minute water touches it—rather like the wicked witch when Dorothy empties the water bucket on her—and I was supposed to attend an official function that evening.

I slid into my car just as the rain started in earnest and there was Reid's car parked by mine, nose to tail, so that we were facing each other. Reid powered down his window. With the rain slanting into his window instead of mine, I did the same.

"Feel like going to Steve's for supper?" he said.

"Not particularly."

My cousin Steve runs a barbecue house down Highway 48, a little ways past the farm, and it's the best barbecue in Colleton County, but I was pigged out at the moment. During election season, that's all they seem to serve at fund-raisers. "Why?"

"No reason. Just thought it might be fun to go by for the singing. Y'all still do that every week?"

"Yes, but that's on Wednesdays."

I almost had to smile. My brothers and cousins and anybody else that's interested get together informally at Steve's after Wednesday night choir practice or prayer meeting to sing and play bluegrass and gospel. It's so country and Reid's so town. He doesn't play an instrument, he doesn't know the words and he's never dropped in when we were jamming except by accident.

"Well, maybe tomorrow night then?"

Rain pelted his face. His tan shirt and brown-striped tie were getting wet, yet he didn't raise his window as he waited for my answer.

It was after five o'clock and I had plans for the

129

evening, so I quit trying to figure out what he really wanted and said, "Sure."

Maybe he'd hit me with it before I had to watch him make a fool of himself at Steve's.

A month earlier, Cyl DeGraffenried and I had been asked to participate in a "Women in Law" forum at Kirkland Prep, an all-female school on the southwest edge of Raleigh. Since Cyl's apartment is on the way, we'd agreed that I'd pick her up early and we'd stop for supper somewhere first.

Cyl and I aren't best friends but we're working on it. Chronologically, she's five years younger. Psychologically, she acts five years older. She thinks my moral standards are too flexible, I think hers are overly rigid. When we argue politics and religion, she accuses me of being a flaming liberal. I *know* she's a social conservative. She's better read and more intellectual than I am, but she also has a dry, self-deprecating wit that keeps me off balance. Most true conservatives can't laugh at themselves—they're too busy pointing a sour finger at the rest of us—so Cyl's mordant sense of humor gives me hope that I'll convert her yet.

I hadn't seen her around the courthouse during the day, but that wasn't unusual. She prosecutes cases all over the district, wherever Doug Woodall sends her, and I'd left a message on her voice mail that I'd be by her place around six.

Her apartment's in one of the new suburban developments that have popped up like dandelions between Garner and Raleigh. A swimming pool and fitness center surrounded by interlocking two-story duplexes that look more like yuppie townhouses than boxy apartments. Attractive low-maintenance landscaping. Tall spindly sticks that will eventually grow into towering shade trees if the whole place isn't first leveled for another mall.

It was still raining when I drove into the parking area in front of Cyl's ground-floor unit. The wind had died, and rain fell straight down from the sodden gray skies with a steady, almost sullen persistence, as if prepared to go on all night long. We'd had so much in the last few weeks that the ground was saturated, the creeks and rivers were swollen and it didn't seem possible that there was any more water left in the clouds.

I did the umbrella maneuver—the one where you crack the car door, cautiously stick the umbrella up into the air and try to get it completely open so you won't get drenched when you step out of the car? I managed to save my blouse, but when I reached back inside the car for my purse, I tipped the umbrella and dumped a gallon of water on my skirt.

One thing about platform shoes though: they do help you walk through shallow puddles without getting your feet wet.

I splashed over to Cyl's door and stood beneath its mini-portico to ring the bell.

No answer.

I rang again, then scanned the parking area as I waited. Yes, there was her car, two spaces over from mine. She was probably on the phone or in the shower.

This time I leaned on the button a full thirty seconds.

Nada.

The curtains were half open but I couldn't see any

131

movement or much else inside the dark interior. On such a dreary late afternoon, her lights should have been on. Was the power out? Maybe the doorbell didn't work? I pounded on the wooden panel, then put my ear close to the door and mashed the doorbell again till I heard endless chimes echo around the rooms inside.

This wasn't like Cyl at all. She's not only punctual, she's usually punctilious.

I darted back to my car and used my flip phone to dial her number. The answering machine kicked in after the first ring and I said, "Cyl? Are you there? Pick up!"

I finally decided that maybe I'd gotten our signals crossed and that she'd probably gone on ahead with someone else.

Instead of a leisurely gossipy supper, I hit the drive-through at Hardee's and ate a chicken sandwich in my car while the rain drummed on the roof and the windows fogged over.

At Kirkland Prep, I joined Judge Frances Tripp, the appeals court judge who administered my oath of office when I was first appointed to the bench, and Lou Ferncliff, one of the highest-paid personal injury attorneys in Raleigh. But no Cyl. The facilitator was head of the social studies department and very p.c. In addition to enlightening the student body with our female insights into the field of law, we were also supposed to be a visual civics lesson: two white women and two African-Americans, colleagues in law and equals under the law.

Cyl DeGraffenried's absence skewed the balance and made the facilitator very unhappy. I wasn't happy either. This was so totally unlike Cyl that I was starting to worry.

Fortunately, Frances and Lou are troupers and had participated in panels like this so many times they could probably do it in their sleep. And I've never been shy about speaking up, so it was a lively discussion.

The students were bright enough to ask intelligent questions and we probably turned a half-dozen of them on to the law. ("Just what this country needs," Lou laughed as the forum broke up around nine-thirty. "More lawyers.")

I probably should have gone on home, but Cyl's apartment was only a couple of miles out of my way and I knew I wouldn't rest easy if I didn't satisfy myself that she was okay.

Her car hadn't been moved and this time I rang that damn bell for almost three solid minutes. Just when I was ready to give up and go call her grandmother, a light came on in the living room and a moment later, the door opened.

"Cyl?"

She looked like hell. Barefooted, wearing nothing but a long pink cotton T-shirt, her eyes were puffy and bloodshot, her face looked bloated, and she had a bad case of bed hair. She blinked at me as if disoriented.

"What's wrong?" I asked, startled by her groggy appearance. "Are you sick?"

She shook her head dazedly. "Deborah? What time is it? Why are you here?"

"The forum," I said. "Supper. Kirkland Prep. Did you forget?"

"Oh, Lordy, was that tonight? What day is it?"

I reached out and touched her forehead, but it was cool to my fingers, so she wasn't running a fever.

"It's Tuesday. When did you last eat?"

"Sunday? Sunday night?" Her shoulders slumped. "Sunday," she moaned.

I propped my dripping umbrella against the wall beneath the skimpy portico and moved past her. "You need food."

She made a gesture of protest but was too dispirited to do more than follow me into her kitchen and watch as I opened cabinets until I found a can of tomato soup.

I dumped it into a saucepan and while that heated, put some cheese on a slice of whole wheat bread and popped it into her toaster oven. "Are you on anything?"

Cyl shook her head, then paused in uncertainty. "Valium? I couldn't sleep. I think I took a couple sometime last night? This morning?"

I poured hot soup into a mug and put it in her hands. "Drink!"

Obediently, she did as I ordered.

Which only confirmed that something was definitely wrong here. No way does a functioning Cyl DeGraffenried take directions from me.

I made a pot of coffee and when it was ready, she drank that, too, and even nibbled at the toasted cheese.

While she ate, I chattered about the forum and how we'd covered for her and how brilliant Frances and Lou and I had been. Eventually, she almost gave a half-smile as the food and caffeine started to kick in a little and I said, "What's going on, Cyl? Something happen at work?"

She shook her head listlessly.

"Something wrong in your family?" So far as I knew, her grandmother was the only family member she truly cared about. "Your grandmother's not sick, is she?"

"No."

In my book, that left only one thing to make a woman like Cyl fall apart. "Who's the man, Cyl, and what's he done?"

A further thought struck me. "Oh jeeze! You're not pregnant, are you?"

"I wish I were!" she burst out passionately. And then her face crumpled.

If those red eyes were any indication, she'd already cried a river of salty tears. I put my arms around her and made comforting noises as she wept again, long hopeless sobs that echoed the rain streaming down her windows.

There was a box of tissues by the kitchen phone and as her emotional storm dwindled, I pulled out a handful and smoothed her hair while she wiped her eyes and blew her nose.

"Sorry," she said at last, making a visible effort to pull herself together. "This is so stupid. I'm sorry I forgot about the forum and thanks for fixing me the soup, Deborah. I'll be all right now."

Not the most tactful brush-off I've ever had. Not going to work either. If I thought she had a girlfriend to call or a sister she'd turn to, I'd have been out of there as soon as she hinted. But Cyl's such a loner, I didn't think it'd be healthy to leave her to keep going

135

round and around in her head as she'd evidently been doing these last two days.

"So when did he dump you?" I poured myself a cup of coffee and topped hers off again. "Sunday? Saturday?"

"How do you know I didn't dump him?" she asked, with a shadow of her old spirit.

"I've dumped and I've been dumped and I know which one makes me want to stay in bed with the covers pulled over my head. It's pretty bad, huh?"

"We were only together twice." Her voice was weary. "The first man I've been with since law school."

Why was I not surprised?

"I didn't want it to happen. Neither of us did. Not with him—not with him married."

Now that *did* surprise me. As many backhanded jabs as she's made at *my* love life, I knew that Cyl's personal code of morality was straight out of the Old Testament. She might be able to rationalize fornication but no way could she do adultery without a heavy load of guilt.

"We didn't realize what was happening until it was too late," she said. "It was just friendship. Talking. A cup of coffee. He helped me through that rough time, the day I found out what happened to Isaac. He was so easy to talk to. Almost like talking to Isaac when I was a little girl. I felt as if there was nothing I couldn't tell him, that he would just listen. Without judging or condemning."

Isaac was Cyl's uncle, a boy who'd been more like an older brother than an uncle, a brother she'd idolized. He disappeared when she was only eight or nine years old and everyone thought he'd fled to Boston without a backward look, which was probably why Cyl had grown up feeling betrayed and abandoned and wary of trusting again. I was there the day she learned how he died, a day of high emotions, another rainy day like this one, with Cyl so full of grief that—

"Ralph Freeman?" I exclaimed.

Cyl looked almost as shocked as I felt. "How did you guess?"

"Hell, I was standing right beside you when you asked him for a ride back into town. He shared his umbrella with you out to the parking lot. I remember asking about his wife and children and he said they were visiting her family back in Warrenton. Is that when it happened?"

"Nothing happened," Cyl protested. "Not that day, anyhow. We just talked. Then, two weeks ago, he came by the office to ask about a man in his church that he was trying to help. A misdemeanor. It was a Friday afternoon. Everyone else was gone. I pulled the shuck to check the charges. He was reading it over my shoulder. I looked up to say something. Our lips were so close. And then they were touching, and then—"

She broke off but I couldn't help wondering. Right there on Doug Woodall's couch?

"We knew it was wrong. But it felt so right." She sighed and shook her head sadly. "We knew we'd sinned, and we said we'd never do it again. But it was like not knowing how hungry you are till you see the food spread out before you and God help us, Deborah, we were both starving. Touching him. Being touched. It was a banquet. Afterwards, I guess we tried to pretend it was a one-time thing. An aberration. We stayed away from each other for a week and then, Saturday morning . . ."

She fell silent for a long moment and tears pooled again in her large brown eyes. "It was even more wonderful," she whispered.

I didn't know Ralph Freeman's wife except by reputation: a God-fearing, commandment-keeping woman who didn't trust white people. I did know his children though, an eleven-year-old son and a seven-year-old daughter who was an engaging little gigglebox. Kids like Stan and Lashanda are one more reason I don't mess with married men.

As if reading my mind, Cyl said, "He has children, a wife, a commitment to Jesus. And he's right. It could jeopardize my job, too. He can't—*we* can't— That's what he came to tell me Sunday night. We can't ever see each other alone again. And he's right. I *know* he's right. But, oh Deborah, how can I stand it?"

And she began to cry again.

CHAPTER 11

Never did a storm work more cruelly.

September 4 (Weds.)
—As of 6 a.m. Hurricane Fran 26° N by 73.9° W.
—Winds at 100 kts. (115 mph)—now a Category 3 hurricane.
—Predicted to hit land sometime tomorrow night.
—Hurricane watch posted last night from Sebastian Inlet, FL to Little River Inlet, SC.
—Evacuating coastal areas of NC, SC & GA.
—Trop. strm. winds 250+ mi. from eye & hurr. winds out 145 mi.—gale-force wind & rain if it hits NC.

Stan Freeman finished jotting his morning notes with a sense of growing excitement. Maybe they'd get a little action this far inland after all.

Certainly his parents seemed concerned when he joined them for breakfast. The kitchen radio was tuned to WPTF's morning weather report. Rain today and more predicted for tomorrow with gusty winds. Unless Hurricane Fran took a sudden sharp turn soon, North Carolina was definitely in for it.

"It's a biggie," Stan told them happily. "Almost three hundred miles across. A lot bigger than Bertha and you saw what *she* did. They're talking winds a hundred and thirty miles an hour! Storm surges twenty feet high! And if it comes in at Wilmington, we might even get tornadoes."

"Stanley!" his mother protested.

"Tornadoes?" Lashanda's eyes widened. "Like Dorothy? Our house will get blown away? Mama?"

"Your brother's talking about 'way down at the coast," Clara said with soothing tones for her daughter and a warning glare for her son. "That's a long way away. And it seems to me, Stanley, that you should be praying the storm passes by instead of hoping it hits and causes so many people grief."

"I'm not wishing them grief, Mama," he protested as the phone rang and his father got up to answer. "I'm just telling you what the weather reports say. I have to keep up with it for my science project. You want me to get a good grade, don't you?"

As he knew it would, citing school as a justification for his excitement somewhat mitigated her displeasure.

"Don't worry, Shandy," he told his little sister. "We'll be safe this far inland."

A drop of milk splashed on Lashanda's skirt and she jumped up immediately for a wet cloth to sponge it off. She was wearing her Brownie uniform since they were meeting immediately after school.

His father hung up the phone and came back to the

table. "That was Brother Todd. He and the other deacons think we ought to cancel prayer meeting tonight, and spend the evening taking down the tent. The canvas is so rain-soaked that it's dripping through. One strong gust could send it halfway to Raleigh."

"When will you start?" asked Stan. "After school? I can help, can't I?"

"Me, too," said Lashanda.

"You're too little," Clara told her. "Besides, that's men's work."

"It's not fair!" Lashanda's big brown eyes started to puddle up. "Boys get to have all the fun."

"I thought we agreed not to stereotype gender roles," Ralph said mildly.

Clara's tone was three shades colder. "Wrestling with a tent in the wind and rain is not appropriate for a little girl."

"Or a little boy either," he said with a smile for his daughter. "But I bet we can find something that *is* appropriate. Maybe you can gather up the tent pegs, honey. Would you like that?"

The child nodded vigorously.

"We'll see," said Clara as the phone rang again.

"For you," Ralph told her, handing over the receiver.

"Sister Clara?" came a woman's strong voice. "This is Grace Thomas and I sure do hate to bother you this early in the morning, but I wanted to catch you 'fore you got off."

Grace Thomas was a fiercely independent old woman who lived a few miles out from Cotton Grove. She and her late husband were childless, her only niece lived in Washington, and there were no near black neighbors. Even the nearest white neighbor was a quarter-mile away. None of this had been a problem until she broke her leg last week.

"You're not bothering me a bit," said Clara. "How's that leg of yours?"

"Well, it's not hurting so bad, but I still can't drive yet and with the hurricane coming and all, I was wondering if maybe you or one of the other sisters could fetch me some things from the store?"

"I'll be happy to." Clara signalled to Stan to hand her the notepad and pencil that lay on the counter.

She was in the habit of listing her plans for the day and the list already had four or five items on it.

Now she added Mrs. Thomas's needs: bread, milk, eggs, cat food, lettuce, lamp oil and a half-dozen C batteries.

"Batteries might not be a bad idea for us," said Ralph as he finished eating and carried his dishes to the sink. "I doubt we'll lose power, but you never know. Best be prepared. Isn't that the Scout motto, Shandy?"

The child wasn't listening. Instead, she wiggled her finger around in her mouth and pulled out something small and white.

"My tooth fell out! Look, Daddy! I wasn't biting down hard or anything and it just fell out. Am I bleeding?"

She bared her teeth and there was a gap in her lower incisors. Three of the upper ones had been shed so long that they were half-grown back in, but this was the first of the lower ones.

"Better hurry up and put it in a glass of water," Stan

teased. "You let it dry out and the Tooth Fairy won't give you more than a nickel for it."

The Tooth Fairy had been yet another of the many forbiddens in Clara's childhood and she was eternally conscious of her father's strictures concerning anything supernatural. Ralph, though, likened it to believing in Santa Claus, just another harmless metaphor for an aspect of God's love. She suspected there was something faulty in his logic—Santa Claus might be an elf, yet he was modeled on a real saint, whereas the Tooth Fairy—? But Ralph had more book-learning and he was her husband, the head of their household, she told herself, and it was her wifely duty to submit to his judgment in these matters. Besides, they'd allowed Stanley to believe and it didn't seem to have interfered with his faith in Jesus.

So her smile was just as indulgent as Ralph's when Lashanda carefully deposited her tooth in a small glass of water and carried it back to her bedroom.

Their shared complicity made it the first time since Sunday that things had felt normal to Stan. His mother's smile transformed her face. Forever after, whenever he remembered that moment, he was always glad that he'd reached out and touched her hand and said, "You look awful pretty today, Mama."

She was usually too self-conscious to accept compliments easily, but today she gently patted his cheek. "Better go brush your teeth, son, or we're going to be late."

When they were alone in the kitchen, Clara lifted her eyes to Ralph in a look that was almost a challenge.

He picked up his umbrella and briefcase. "I'll be

home by four-thirty," he said as he went out to the carport.

In the days to come, it would be his burden that there had been no love in his heart for her this morning.

That he hadn't said, "Your mama *does* look pretty today."

That he hadn't even said goodbye.

"Hello? . . . Hello?" The man's voice became impatient. "Is anybody there? Hello!"

The rain was coming down hard, drumming on her red umbrella like the racing of her heart. Rosa Edwards swallowed hard and tried to speak, but she was so nervous, she knew she'd botch it.

Instead, she abruptly hung up and moved away from the exposed public telephone outside the convenience store. She had thought out everything she meant to say, but the minute she heard his voice, knowing he was a murderer, she couldn't speak.

Telephones were so fancy these days. Buttons you could push and it'd call the person you last called. Another button and it'd tell you what number last called you. Not that it'd get him anywhere if he did find out she was calling from this phone. Wasn't in her neighborhood.

Her feet were soaking wet as she splashed back to her raggedy old car that just came out of the shop for $113.75. While rain beat against the piece of plastic she'd taped over the broken window on the passenger side, she rehearsed it in her mind all again, the way she'd just say it right out, no messing around. Then, when she was perfectly calm, she walked back to the phone, inserted her coins and dialed his number again.

As soon as he answered, she spoke his name and said, "This is the gal that saw you coming out of Room 130 at the Orchid Motel Saturday evening."

First he tried to bluster, then he tried to intimidate her, but she plowed on with what she had to say.

"Now you just hush up and listen. What you done to her ain't nothing to do with me. You give me ten thousand dollars cash money and I won't never say nothing to nobody. You don't and I'm going straight to the police. You get the money together and I'll call you back this number at six o'clock and tell you where to leave it."

She hung up without giving him a chance to answer, and even though the concrete was wet and her tires were almost bald, she laid down rubber getting out of the parking lot just in case there were fancier, quicker ways to find out where she was calling from.

The rain was starting to get on Norwood Love's nerves. The young man had worked his muscles raw these last few days, trying to get this underground chamber fitted out properly with running water, drainage pipes, air-conditioning, propane tanks, and ventilation ducts. His cousin Sherrill had helped some. Sherrill was the only one he trusted to help and keep his mouth closed. Most of it, he'd done alone though, keeping it secret even from his wife. Not many women want their husbands to mess with whiskey and JoAnn was no different. Fortunately, she worked regular hours in town, so it wasn't all that hard to do things without her noticing.

With the money from Kezzie Knott, he'd bought some stainless steel vats second-hand at a soup factory over in Harnett County. He'd fashioned the cooker to his own design, did the welding himself. The copper condensing coil was one his dad had made before he flipped out the last time—*Only thing he ever give me that he didn't take back soon as he sobered up,* thought Norwood. The fifty-gallon plastic barrels from that pickle factory out near Goldsboro stood clean and ready to fill.

He knew how to buy sugar in bulk without getting reported and he had a couple of migrant crew bosses waiting to buy whenever he was ready to sell.

Best of all, he'd figured out a way to keep the smell of fermenting mash from giving him away. That's how most ALE officers claimed they stumbled over a lot of stills, just following their noses. In his personal opinion, that was a bunch of bull. Oh, maybe once in a blue moon, it'd happen like that. Most times, though, it was somebody talking out of turn or talking for bounty money. All the same, for that one chance in a hundred, he meant not to be found by any smells.

But this rain! The dirt floor was turning into a mudpie and water was seeping down the concrete block walls. And now the weatherman was saying hurricane? Be a hell of a note if he got flooded out before he even got started good.

To Rosa Edwards's relief, she hadn't left it too late. The Freeman children were just coming out to the carport when she got there. She pulled her car in beside Clara's and hopped out, leaving the motor running. "Your mama inside?"

"Yes, ma'am," said Lashanda.

"We're on our way to school," Stan warned her.

"It's okay," said Rosa. "I won't make y'all late."

She darted on into the house just as Clara came down the hall with her purse in one hand and car keys in the other.

"Rosa! Good morning." She tilted her head in concern. "Is something wrong?"

"No, no, and I know you're in a hurry. I got one quick little favor to ask you though."

"It'll have to be real quick," Clara said, glancing at the kitchen clock. "I forgot how rain slows everything down."

Rosa handed her the white envelope she carried. Humidity made the paper limp, but it was sealed with Scotch tape.

"Would you keep this for me?"

The envelope wasn't thick. No more than a single sheet of paper inside. Clara turned it in her hand and looked at Rosa inquiringly.

"I can't tell you what it is," said Rosa. "But would you just hold on to it for me till I ask for it back? Keep it somewhere safe?"

"Sure," said Clara and tucked it in her purse as she shepherded Rosa toward the door. "I'll keep it right here next to my billfold."

"Thanks," Rosa said, heading for her own shabby car which waited with the motor still running. "See you tonight."

Then she was gone before Clara remembered to tell her that prayer meeting was going to be cancelled.

*   *   *

"Millard King? Yes, I know him," said the librarian. "Well, not *know* him, but I know who he is. Why?"

Deputy Mayleen Richards smiled encouragingly. "He said you passed him out on the track at the Dobbs middle school Saturday afternoon."

Peggy Lasater wrinkled her forehead in an effort to remember.

"He said you were wearing red shorts and a white shirt."

"Did he happen to mention that I was also wearing a Walkman?"

Richards checked her notes. "No Walkman."

"People think if you're a librarian, you spend your days reading. They should see all the shelving and cataloging we do. When I run? That's when I get to read."

"Read?"

The librarian nodded. "Books on tape. I did run Saturday afternoon, but I was too absorbed in the last Charlotte MacLeod to notice anything except where I was putting my feet. Sorry."

Clara Freeman left Cotton Grove and drove south on Old 48, a narrow winding road that follows the meanders of Possum Creek. With headlights and wipers both on high, she drove cautiously through the heavy rain. Where the road dipped, deep puddles had formed. They sent up broad wings of water on either side of her Civic as she plowed through.

Once beyond the city limits, there were few cars on the road and she was able to relax a bit and to open her window a tiny crack. Not enough to let the rain in, but

enough to keep the windshield from fogging up so
badly.

She had dropped the children off at school, taken
Brother Wilkins to the eye clinic, picked up the dry
cleaning, waited for Brother Wilkins to come out of
the clinic, taken him to the Winn-Dixie with her while
she shopped for Sister Grace, then helped him into the
house with his few bags of groceries. ("Bless you,
child," he'd said. "I'm gonna pray God sends you help
in your old age like He sent you to help us.")

She would deliver Sister Grace's things and then it
would be time for lunch. After lunch—?

Her mind momentarily blanked on what came next
on the list.

As Ralph's wife—no, as the *minister's* wife—she had
cheerfully put her services at the beck and call of his
congregation and she'd always made lists to organize
her days. But since finding those condoms in his desk
on Sunday, she tried to pack her days even fuller so she
wouldn't have time to brood on how his betrayal un-
dermined the very foundation on which she'd built
her life.

Her hands gripped the steering wheel so fiercely
that her knuckles gleamed through the tight skin.

How? she asked herself for the thousandth time
since she'd found those condoms. How *could* he have
done this dreadful, stupid thing? Did every man, from
the President of the United States of America right
down to her own husband, put sex before honor?
Make themselves slaves of their malehood, shackle
their God-given free will to their gonads?

At least Ralph didn't try to excuse himself by saying,
"The woman tempted me so I sinned." No, he'd

rightfully taken the blame on himself. And when he came back home Sunday night and lay down beside her in the darkness, she'd asked two questions. "Does she go to our church?"

"No," he'd answered.

"Is she white?"

"No, Clara."

That was all she'd wanted to know, but he had a question of his own. "Do you want a divorce?"

Her heart leaped up and she'd let Satan tempt her for a moment.

To be free of him always wanting what she didn't have in her to give? To go back to her father's house? To sleep alone in a narrow bed?

Then she remembered being a daughter in her father's house, a minister's daughter, not a minister's wife. Abiding by rules, not making them. Having to ask, not tell.

As a wife, she had the power to do God's work.

As a daughter? A divorced woman with a failed marriage?

Her father would do his duty by her, however much he might disapprove of her decision. His congregation would be kind.

But respect? Position?

"No," she'd said. "No, I don't want a divorce. All I want is your promise that you'll never go to her again."

"As God is my strength," he told her.

She had turned to him then, ready to give her body as a reward for his vow. He had not pushed her away, merely patted her shoulder as if she were Lashanda or Stanley. In that moment, she realized that he might never again reach for her in the night, and part of her was glad.

Another part felt suddenly bereft.

That sense of loss still clung to her this morning even though she knew that she'd acted as God would have her. She had been grievously wronged, yet she had risen above his sin. She had forgiven him. So why should *she* feel this inner need for forgiveness?

With relief, she reached the dead end of the unpaved road where Sister Thomas lived and hurried inside with the groceries and supplies.

She fed Sister Thomas's cat, changed the sheets on the bed and straightened up the kitchen, but when the old woman invited her to stay for lunch, she excused herself and ran through the rain back to her car.

In just the hour that she'd been inside, the rutted clay roadbed had turned into a slippery, treacherous surface that scared her as the tires lost traction and kept skewing toward the deep ditches. She was perspiring freely by the time she'd driven the quarter-mile back to the hardtop.

Pulling out onto the paved road, she recklessly lowered her window and let the cool rain blow in her face. She took deep breaths of the humid air that did nothing to dislodge the weight that seemed to have settled on her heart since Sunday night.

That's when she noticed the lights of a car behind her. Even though it was noon, the sky was black and the dazzle of lights on her rain-smeared rear window made it impossible for her to distinguish make or driver. Dark and late-model were all she could tell about the car as it rushed up behind her.

She moved over to the right as far as possible. If he

was in that big a hurry, maybe he'd go ahead and pass even though there were double yellow lines on this twisty stretch.

A second later, her head jerked and she felt her car being bumped from behind.

What the—?

Another glance in the rearview mirror. He'd done it deliberately! And now he was so close that the head-lights were blanked out by the rear of her own car.

She could clearly see the white man behind the steering wheel.

Fear grabbed her and she stepped on the accelerator.

He bumped her again.

It was her worst nightmare unfolding in daylight.

Her dress was getting soaked, but she was too terri-fied to think of raising the window. Instead, she floored the gas pedal and the Civic leaped forward.

Almost instantly, he caught up with her.

The road curved sharply and she nearly lost control as the car fishtailed on the wet pavement.

Then he pulled even with her and they raced through the rain, neck and neck along the deserted road and through another lazy S-curve that swept down to an old wooden bridge over Possum Creek. With so much rain, the creek had overflowed its banks and was almost level with the narrow bridge.

Again Clara pulled to the right to give him room to pass.

At that instant, he bumped her so hard from the side that her air bag inflated. She automatically braked, but it was too late. The Civic was airborne and momentum carried it straight into the creek. By the time it hit the water, the air bag had deflated and Clara's head cracked hard against the windshield, sending her into darkness.

As the car sank deeper, muddy creek water flooded through the open window.

Just as he was thinking about lunch, Dwight Bryant looked up to see Deputy Richards hovering near his door and he motioned her in.

"I spoke to the librarian that Millard King said was jogging when he was. She was listening to a book on her Walkman and couldn't say who else was out there."

"Too bad. But King said he thought one of the men was a doctor. Try calling around to see if any of them were jogging."

"Yes, sir. And remember that jewelry store manager who bought the other two silver pens?"

"New Orleans, right? You talked to her?"

"Yes, sir, but no help there. She gave those two pens to her granddaughters. They're in high school in New Mexico and still have them so far as she knows."

Dwight frowned. "I knew it wasn't going to be that easy."

"No, sir," said Mayleen Richards. "I'll start calling the doctors."

When his phone rang promptly at six p.m., he was momentarily startled, but he collected himself in the next instant and his voice was calm. "Hello?"

"It's me," said the woman.

The same woman who'd called this morning.

The woman he'd sent crashing into the creek at noon.

Wasn't it?

"You got the ten thousand?"

"Who is this?" he croaked.

"You know who it is," she answered impatiently. "You got the money or do I go to the police?"

"How do I know you won't anyhow?"

"'Cause I'm giving you my word and I ain't never broke my word yet."

Like I'd trust you far as I could throw you, he thought angrily.

But he willed himself to calmness. He was an educated white man, he told himself, and she was a stupid black bitch. He'd already killed one nigger woman today. He could certainly kill another.

"I've got the money," he lied. "Where do you want to meet?"

"We ain't gonna meet." Tersely, she named the Dobbs Public Library, told him to put the money inside a white plastic bag, and described where he was to leave the packet in precisely forty-five minutes. "I'll be watching. You leave it and just walk on out the front door, 'cause I see your face I'm gonna start screaming the walls down."

That didn't give him much time to fashion a packet that looked like money, wrapped tightly in a plastic bag and wound around with duct tape. She might duck into the ladies' room, but she'd never get into this packet without a knife or scissors. Satisfied, he put the packet into a white plastic bag as instructed, drove to the library, left it on the floor beside the specified chair, and walked out without looking back.

Once outside though, he raced around the corner, through the alley and back to his car that he'd left parked well down the block. A few minutes later, through his rain-streaked windshield, he saw a black woman emerge from the library with her large hand-bag clutched to her chest. From this distance, she looked only vaguely like the Freeman woman he'd been following all week. Not that he'd paid all that much attention. It wasn't the woman he'd followed, so much as the car.

But who the hell was this woman?

Whoever she was, she hurried through the rain to a junker car that looked like it was on its last legs. This was the tricky part. Did she have something in the car to cut open the packet? And if she did, would she go straight to the police or would she try to call him again?

Neither, he realized as she headed out of town toward Cotton Grove. Dobbs's rush hour was nothing compared to Raleigh's, but he was able to keep one or two cars back as they drove westward.

Stupid bitch.

The weather station's announcer was going crazy with excitement as Fran appeared to draw a bead on the Carolinas. Stan dutifully noted the huge storm's position—it was something to do to pass the time—but his head wasn't into his science project this evening.

Not with Mama missing.

It wasn't unusual to come home and find her not there.

It *was* unusual to get a call from Lashanda's Brownie leader asking if Mrs. Freeman had forgotten to pick her up.

If it hadn't been raining so hard, he'd have ridden

his bicycle over to get her himself. As it was, he'd called his dad.

"I'm on my way, son, but how about you phone over to Sister Edwards's house and see if Mama's there?"

"Sorry, honey," Miss Rosa had said. "I haven't talked to her since this morning."

He remembered Mrs. Thomas's grocery list and called there, but with no better results. By the time Dad's car rolled into the yard with Lashanda, Stan was starting to get worried.

Now it was heading for dark and still no news of Mama.

As word spread through their church, the phone rang frequently, all with the same soft questions: "Sister Clara home yet? Well now, don't you children fret. I'm sure she'll turn up just fine."

When Lashanda's best friend, Angela Herbert, arrived with her mother shortly before seven, Stan had protested. "We don't need a babysitter. I'm almost twelve years old, Dad. I can take care of Lashanda."

"I know you can, son, but your sister's only seven and having a friend here will make it easier on her."

"Then let me come with you," he'd pleaded.

"It would help me more to know you're here answering the phone in case Mama calls," his father said.

Unhappily, Stan watched his father leave through the rain. He sure hoped Mama was somewhere safe and dry.

When the junker car pulled into the yard of a shabby little house at the end of the road, he realized that this was where he'd seen the driver of the Honda Civic drop someone off yesterday morning.

It was instantly clear to him that he'd made a colossal mistake, but instead of remorse, he felt only anger at the woman who was now entering this house without a backward glance. How could he have known? Not his fault that two different women were both driving the same car.

The road curved behind a thick clump of sassafras and wild cherry trees and he pulled his car up close to them, trusting to twilight, the rain and the house's isolation to help him.

Inside, he saw the woman sawing at his packet with a paring knife. The screen door was hooked, but he put his fist right through the rusted mesh and flipped up the hook.

Rosa Edwards turned with a start and screamed as he burst into the room. She held the puny little knife before her, but he backhanded her so hard that the knife went flying and she fell heavily against the table.

He hit her again and blood gushed from her split lips.

"You better not!" she whimpered, scrabbling across the floor as she tried to get away. "I wrote it down. Somebody's got the paper, too!"

"Who?" he snarled and kicked her hard in the stomach.

"I don't get it back, she'll read it!" Her words came raggedly as she gasped for air. "She'll know you the one done it."

Enraged, he grabbed her by the hair and half-lifted her from the floor as he punched her in the face again. "Who, you bitch? Who you give it to?"

"I ain't telling!" she sobbed.

"Oh yes, you will! Yes, you damn well will."

Still holding her by the hair, he dragged her over to the kitchen counter and started opening drawers till he found a butcher knife.

"You tell me where that paper is or I'm gonna start cutting off fingers, one finger at a time, and then I'm gonna work on your tits. You hear me?"

Desperately, she struggled against him, but he grabbed her arm and twisted it behind her so viciously that she heard the bone snap.

CHAPTER | 12

The twisting tornado is confined to a narrow track and it has no long-drawn-out horrors. Its climax is reached in a moment. The hurricane, however, grows and grows.

It was nearly five before I adjourned court on Wednesday after hearing a silly case that took longer than any of the combatants (and I use the term advisedly) expected. Reid Stephenson was representing a young man who seemed to think he could race his motorcycle engine in front of his ex-girlfriend's house in the middle of the night as long as he didn't actually speak to her or threaten her or come onto her property or get within thirty feet of her as an earlier judgment had enjoined him from doing.

Reid tried to argue that it was only when the young woman came to her window to yell obscenities that the thirty-foot prohibition was violated. In other words, his client got there first and it was the girl-friend who chose to step outside her perimeter. Long-suffering neighbors who called the police wanted a larger perimeter around both of them. I decided they had a point and told the young man he might have obeyed the letter of the law, but I was going to let him sit in jail for three days and think about the spirit.

Despite my ruling, Reid came up to me as I was leaving the courtroom and said, "So how 'bout I pick you up around eight?"

"You're really serious about going to Steve's this evening?"

"Well, sure I am," he said. "Good barbecue? A chance to see the boys, catch up with them?"

Reid was Mother's first cousin, so he's known my brothers all his life, but being a lot younger and growing up in town to boot, it's not like as if they were close or anything, although he used to trail along when his father came out to the farm to hunt or fish.

When Reid passed the bar, Brix Jr. cut him a piece of the firm and retired to fish and play golf full-time. That's when Daddy switched over to John Claude for all his legal needs. Out of loyalty, most of the boys gave me their business while I was in practice there and they still use Lee and Stephenson. They'll even turn to Reid in an emergency—when the kids get in trouble and John Claude's out of town—but like Daddy, they feel safer with John Claude.

In short, Reid does not have a particularly warm and fuzzy ongoing relationship with my brothers, so why this sudden urge to (as Haywood would say) fellow-ship with them when rain was falling and a hurricane was heading toward our coastline?

Come eight o'clock though, there he was, rapping on my side door. I'd left my two-car garage open so he could drive in out of the rain. He still had on his gray suit but he held a hanger in one hand, slacks and knit shirt in the other.

"Didn't have time to change," he said. "Borrow your bedroom?"

Since I'd sort of flung things around when I went from dress and pantyhose to jeans and sneakers, I pointed him to the guest room instead. While he changed, I neatened my bedroom, hung up clothes and straightened all the surfaces. Maidie's promised to find me someone to do the heavy scrubbing and vacu- uming one morning a week, but she hasn't gotten to it yet.

When Reid came out, I handed him my guitar case and went around locking doors, something he watched with amusement.

"You don't need to worry about burglars out here in the middle of Knott land, do you?"

"I'm not so worried about burglars as I am about Knotts," I said lightly.

Half my brothers think nothing of opening an un- locked door and sometimes they're just a little too cu- rious about my personal business. Seth and Maidie are the only ones I trust with a key, which is why I'm try- ing to get in the habit of locking up every time I leave. I pulled the side door closed behind us and made sure it was securely latched.

"What happened to your fender?" I asked as I cir- cled the front of Reid's black BMW.

It had a serious dent just behind the right headlight.

"Damned if I know," he said. "I found it like that

161

after court yesterday. Two days out of the shop and somebody backs into me. Didn't even have the courtesy to leave me his name."

Considering a courthouse parking lot's clientele, this did not exactly surprise me. What did surprise was that he wasn't bitching about it louder. Reid's as car proud as my nephews and with a five-hundred deductible, every little ding comes out of his pocket.

Rain was falling heavily again and my rutted drive had washed out in a couple of places so that we had to go slower than usual to ease over the humps. We didn't get to Steve's till almost eight-thirty.

Despite the pounds of barbecue I'd eaten in the last month, that tangy smell of vinegar and smoked pork did make me hungry. We sat down at a long wooden table where Haywood and Isabel were finishing up and we both ordered the usual: pig, cole slaw, spiced apples and hushpuppies. We even split a side order of fried chicken livers. (Yeah, yeah, we've both heard all the horror stories of cholesterol and mercury in organ meat, but Miss Ila, Steve's seventy-year-old cook, knows how to make them crispy on the outside and melt-in-your-mouth-moist on the inside and neither of us can believe something that good can do lasting hurt if you don't indulge too often.)

Except for Steve, Miss Ila and a dishwasher, we four were the only ones in the place till Andrew's Ruth and Zach's Lee and Emma came dripping in from choir practice a few minutes later and ordered a helping of banana pudding with three spoons.

"We just came by to tell y'all we can't stay," said Ruth, pushing back her damp hair. "Mom's worried about the roads flooding."

"The water was almost hubcap-deep at Pleasants Crossroads," said Lee, "but that ol' four-by-four's better'n a duck. We won't have any trouble getting home."

All the usual customers had scattered earlier and it was clear that the rest of our families were staying home, battening down miscellaneous hatches in case we got any of Fran in the next twenty-four hours. Aunt Sister had already called to say that none of her crowd would be coming. When the kids left, Miss Ila and her helper were right in behind them. Steve put the CLOSED sign up, but we didn't reach for our instruments. Instead, we talked about Fran and what more rain would do to our already-saturated area, amusing each other with worst-case scenarios in half-serious tones, the way you will when you're fairly confident that any actual disaster will bypass you. Hurricanes do hit our coast with monotonous regularity, but this far inland, we seldom get much fallout beyond some heavy downpours.

Crabtree Valley Mall was built on a flood plain and it does indeed flood every three or four years. (The local TV stations love to film all the new cars bobbing around the sales lots like corks on a fish pond.)

Bottomland crops may drown when the creeks overflow, a few trees go down and mildew is a constant annoyance, but most storms blow out before they reach us.

"Don't forget Hazel," said Isabel.

As if.

Hazel slammed through here in the mid-fifties before Reid and I were born, but we've been hearing about it every hurricane season since we were old enough to know what a hurricane was. Each year, I have to listen to tales of porches torn off houses, doing without electricity for several days, and about the millions of dollars' worth of damage it did. Down in the woods, there are still huge trees that blew over then but didn't die. Now, all along the leaning trunks, limbs have grown up vertically to form trees on their own.

"Hazel knocked that 'un down," a brother will tell me as he launches into stream-of-consciousness memories of that storm.

"It hit here in the middle of the day while we was still in school," said Haywood, warming to his tale like the Ancient Mariner.

"Back then, they didn't close school for every little raindrop nor snowflake neither," said Isabel, singing backup.

"They should've that day though. Remember how the sky got black and the wind come up?"

"And little children were crying?"

"Blew past in a hurry, but even the principal was worried and he called the county superintendent and they turned us out soon as it was past."

"Trees and light poles down across the road," said Isabel. "Our school bus had to go way outten the way to get us all home and we younguns had to walk in from the hardtop almost half a mile on that muddy road."

"Daddy and Mama Sue—"

Haywood was interrupted by a sharp rap on the restaurant's front door.

We looked over to see a tall dark figure standing in the rain.

Steve signalled that he was closed, but the man rapped again.

The glass was fogged up too much to see exactly who it was. I was nearest the door and as much to end Haywood's remembrances of Hazel as anything else, I went and opened it to find Ralph Freeman.

He was soaking wet and obviously worried, although he managed one of those bone-warming smiles the instant he recognized me.

"Come on in," I said. "Steve, Haywood, Reid—y'all know Reverend Freeman, don't you? Preaches at Balm of Gilead?"

They made welcoming sounds, but Ralph didn't advance past the entryway.

"Sorry to bother you," he said, dripping on the welcome mat, "but it's my wife. She was out this way today, visiting Mrs. Grace Thomas, and I was wondering if any of y'all saw her? White Honda Civic? Sister Thomas says my wife left her house a little after twelve and nobody's seen her since."

"Grace Thomas," said Haywood. "She live on that road off Old Forty-eight, right before Jones Chapel?"

"That's right," Ralph said, turning to him eagerly. "Did you see her?"

Haywood shook his head. "Naw. Sorry."

The others were shaking their heads, too.

"I just don't know where she could be," said Ralph. "I thought maybe she'd had a flat tire. Or with all this rain, these deep puddles, she might've drowned out the engine. But I've been up and down almost every road between here and Cotton Grove."

"I'll call around," said Haywood, heading for the phone. "See if any of the family's seen her car."

"Did you call the sheriff's department?" I asked.

"They said she's not been gone long enough for them to do anything official, but they did say they'd keep an eye out for the car."

"Highway patrol?" Reid suggested.

"Same thing," he answered dispiritedly. "And I've called all the hospitals."

"Now don't you go thinking the worst," Isabel comforted. "She could've slid into a ditch and she's either waiting for someone to find her or she's holed up in somebody's house that doesn't have a telephone."

Ralph looked dubious. "I doubt that. She doesn't know anybody else out this way and she wouldn't walk up to a stranger's house."

A tactful way to put it. Knowing that Mrs. Freeman disliked whites almost as much as certain whites dislike blacks, I figured he was right. She probably wouldn't want to chance it with any of us.

Nor was Ralph much comforted by Isabel's suggestion that she could be waiting out the rain in the car somewhere. Not when we were due for a whole lot more if Fran kicked in as weathermen were predicting.

Haywood came back from the telephone shaking his head. "Everybody's sticking close to home and ain't seen no cars in the ditch or nothing. Sorry, Preacher. But we'll surely keep our eyes peeled going home. Which ought to be about now, don't you reckon, Bel?" he asked.

She nodded and came heavily to her feet. She's only about half Haywood's size, but since he's just over six feet tall and just under three hundred pounds, that still makes her a hefty woman by anybody's standards.

"Such a shame we couldn't do any picking and

singing tonight," she lamented, reaching for her banjo case. "Maybe next week we'll have more folks to come. You know, we might need to start us a phone tree to turn us out better." As she passed Ralph, she said, "I sure hope Miz Freeman makes it home safe. This is real bad weather to get stuck off somewhere."

We all said goodnight to Steve, who locked up behind us and turned off the lights on his way through the restaurant to the rear door that's a shortcut to his house out back.

Haywood held an umbrella over Isabel as they splashed out to their car. Like the southern gentleman he aspires to become, Reid told me to stay under the porch while he brought the car over.

Ralph Freeman stood beside me staring out at the rain indecisively. His face held the same hopeless misery I'd seen on Cyl's face last night, and to my horror, instead of some innocuous platitude about hoping everything turned out okay, I heard myself say, "Did y'all have a fight? Is she doing this deliberately? Punishing you for Cyl?"

"Cyl?" The worry lines between his eyes deepened. "You mean Ms. DeGraffenried?"

I touched his arm. "You don't have to pretend, Ralph. I know about you two."

"You do?" He looked at me warily. "How? She tell you?"

"Only after I guessed," I said and told him how I'd put two and two together last night.

"How is she?" His need was so great that it was almost as if he didn't care that I knew so long as I could tell him about Cyl.

"She's really hurting."

His broad shoulders slumped even more if that was possible.

Reid pulled in beside the single porch step. I held up two fingers and he cut his lights to show that he'd wait with his motor running till I finished talking.

Ralph said, "You must think I'm the world's biggest hypocrite."

"It's not for me to judge," I answered primly.

"No?" He gave me such an ironic lift of his eyebrow that I had to smile.

"You know what I mean. I've got too much glass in my own house for me to go around looking for stones in my neighbors' eyes."

That didn't come out quite the way I intended, although Haywood would surely have understood my mangled metaphors.

"Where are your children?" I asked pointedly.

"Home. The wife of one of our deacons is with them. And to answer your first question, Clara might do something like this to me, but she'd never do it to them. She was supposed to pick Lashanda up from her Brownie meeting after school, but she didn't. I can't understand it."

"Friends?" I said. "Family?"

"All back in Warrenton except for her prayer partner. Rosa's the only one Clara's really taken to since we moved here. Rosa Edwards. I called her right off, but she hasn't seen Clara since first thing this morning. I don't know where else to look, who else to call."

"Maybe you just ought to go on home," I said. "Be with the children. That's where she'd call, wouldn't she?"

He nodded. "She'll know they're worried and she'll want them to know she's all right, soon as possible."

"Want me to speak to Dwight Bryant? He could probably put on a couple of extra patrol cars."

"Would you? I'd appreciate that." He hesitated. "You wouldn't have to tell him about Cyl and me, would you?"

"Of course not."

"Thanks, Deborah."

"No problem," I said.

He took a deep breath and stepped out bareheaded into the rain. Reid pushed open the passenger door and I slid inside.

As we headed back down 48, Reid said, "What was that all about?"

"His wife. He's really worried about her."

With Ralph's red taillights shining up ahead, we rode in a silence broken only by the windshield wipers on wet glass, till Reid turned off the highway onto the road that led to my house. I found myself automatically checking the ditches on both sides, half-expecting to see Clara Freeman's car.

When we got to my house, I pushed the remote and once more the garage door swung up so that Reid could drive in.

"Any chance of a cup of coffee?" he asked.

"Sure," I replied. "Just let me call Dwight first."

I could have called from the kitchen, of course; instead, I went straight to the phone beside my bed. Sometimes Dwight'll give me a hard time for meddling. Tonight he listened as I stated the case against

Clara Freeman just taking off without a thought for her children.

"Ralph's afraid she's had a wreck or something and if she has, you know the quicker she gets help, the better it'll be," I urged. "Do you really have to wait twenty-four hours?"

"Okay, okay," he said. "I'll shift all the patrols over to that sector till they've covered all the roads. If she's out there, they'll find her."

Reid was aimlessly opening cabinet doors when I got back to the kitchen.

"Coffee's in the refrigerator," I told him.

"Of course. The one place I didn't look."

He put two filters in the basket—"Cuts the caffeine and acids"—scooped in the ground coffee and flicked the switch.

"Does that weather board I gave you work okay?"

"Sure," I said, though truth to tell, I'd barely glanced at it since he hung it up.

"Let's see how low the pressure is right now with all this rain."

He headed for my bedroom and I trailed along at his heels. Did I mention that all good lawyers are actors? Reid was giving a charming performance at the moment—burbling about how his dad still checks the barometer every morning even though he can now look out the window overlooking the ninth green and see for himself whether it's a good day for golf.

" 'Course with Dad, any day it's not sleeting is a good day for golf."

Once inside my bedroom, he went right over to the

dials and started reading them off. I just leaned against the doorjamb and watched him.

He turned around. "Aren't you interested?"

"Oh, I'm interested all right," I said wickedly. "Since you haven't been able to get back here alone, what did you plan to do? Slide it under my bed as soon as I came over to look? Hope I'd think it rolled there by accident?"

"Huh?"

A textbook look of puzzled innocence spread across his face.

"Considering that it got you off the hook with Dwight, I really think you should have given me something nicer for my wall than a twenty-dollar weather center."

He gave a sheepish grin, his first honest expression of the night. "Wal-Mart doesn't offer a lot of choice. It was this or a sunburst clock or a bad knockoff of a Bob Timberlake painting."

Overall, I had to agree with his decision. Nevertheless, I held out my hand and he reached into his pocket and pulled out the sterling silver pen that he'd lifted from the pencil mug beside my phone on Monday.

"When did you miss it?" he asked, turning the gleaming shaft in his fingers.

"While you were changing clothes tonight, I tidied up in here."

"Well, damn! You mean I was that close to getting away with it?"

"Not really. I knew you were up to something, I just hadn't figured out what. You hate gospel music, remember?"

He shrugged. "I was hoping you wouldn't."

"No more games," I said sternly. "How did your pen get under Lynn Bullock's body?"

"I don't know, Deborah, and that's the God-honest truth. She borrowed it the last time we were together and didn't give it back and, well, it seemed a little petty to make a big point about it since I didn't want to see her again anyhow."

"So why didn't you just tell Dwight?"

"Oh, sure. My pen under the body of a woman whose neck I'd threatened to wring?"

"What?"

"I didn't mean it," he said hastily. "You know how you say things—'I'll kill him,' 'I'm going to clean his clock'? It's just talk. But I was so mad when I saw what she'd done to my car. Hot as it's been? And with the windows rolled up? I had to go buy a pair of rubber gloves just to drive it to the shop. I was so pissed, I kept saying that I was going to wring the little bitch's neck. Everybody at the shop just laughed at me, they didn't have a clue who I was talking about, but Will was there and I'm pretty sure he knew because he gave me a wink and said he'd swear it was justifiable homicide."

If my brother had known Lynn Bullock was the woman who'd done something like that to Reid's car, he certainly would have mentioned it Sunday night when we were talking about her death. Will's a consummate con man though, and he can be incredibly sneaky when he puts his mind to it. He has a way of pretending he knows more about things than he does, hoping to bluff you into telling him what you assume he already knows.

"Don't you see? If Dwight knew it was my pen, he'd go digging around and find out—"

"And find out what?" I asked. Then it hit me. "Wait a minute! You had two dates with her last Christmas and she only lately fouled your car? When?"

"Tuesday, a week ago," he admitted.

"Why?" I asked, even though that mulish look on his face gave me the answer. "Oh for God's sake, Reid! Tell me you didn't. You said she wasn't your type."

"Well, she wasn't," he said sulkily. "All the same, for all her snob talk, there was something—I don't know—vulnerable? Did I tell you what she said about Dad coming out to her grandfather's place when she was a little girl?"

"No."

"She was just a kid when it happened, but she never forgot. Dad had gone out to coach her grandfather for a court appearance. She talked about Dad's fingernails. How clean and even they were."

Reid looked down at his own neatly manicured nails and I had a sudden mental image of my daddy's hands, the nails split and stained with country work.

"What was her grandfather charged with?"

"I looked it up in the files." Reid gave me a lopsided grin. "Let's put it this way. Your dad was paying my dad's bill. *And* he paid her grandfather's fine and court costs."

"*What?*"

"Oh, come on, Deb'rah. Everybody knows Mr. Kezzie made his money in bootleg whiskey."

"When he was younger, yes," I agreed, "but he gave all that up before I was born and Lynn Bullock was younger than me."

"Whiskey's the only thing your daddy's ever lied to me about," Mother once told me. "The only thing I *know* he lied about anyhow."

I looked at Reid sharply. "Is he still mixed up in it?"

"Old as he is? I doubt it," said Reid. " 'Course, a lot of people still think he is, and it probably amuses him to let them. I'm sure you'd've heard about it, if he were."

"True," I said, relieved. Dwight or Terry or certainly Ed Gardner, who works ATF, would have put a bug in my ear if he were still active. One thing a judge doesn't need is to have her daddy hauled in for making moonshine.

"Anyhow," said Reid, "Lynn Bullock was a damn good lay. I'm not seeing anybody special these days, so I thought what the hell, why not give her another call?"

"Only her memory being better than yours, she was still ticked that you'd dumped her after the second night and it really steamed her when you called out of the blue with nothing on your mind but sex?"

"Something like that. Look, Deborah, you've got to help me. Don't tell Dwight it was your pen I showed him. Okay?"

"You're crazy. I'm a judge. An officer of the court. I can't *not* tell him. So she smeared dog dirt inside your car. Big deal. And you vented at the garage. Hyperbole. You tell him who you were with before you got to the ball field, she confirms it and—"

There was that look again. "No who?"

"No who," he said.

"You're not being noble, are you?" I asked suspiciously. "Saving somebody's reputation?"

"The only reputation I was saving was mine. Everybody thinks I get laid six days a week and twice on Sundays. Truth is, I'm damn near a virgin these days. I went to the office Saturday morning, got sleepy after lunch, flaked out upstairs and almost slept through the game."

I looked at him. I may have eleven older brothers, but he's the nearest thing to a kid brother I'd ever had. His handsome face was an open book.

Or was it?

"Oh come on, Deborah. I did *not* kill Lynn Bullock."

"You know he couldn't," whispered my internal preacher.

"Irrelevant!" snapped the pragmatist from the other side of my head. "You withhold something like this from Dwight and you could find yourself facing an ethics review."

Reid still held my pen in his hand.

"If I'd been a little smarter, I'd have found a way to put this back and you wouldn't have known the difference. All you have to do is forget the last few minutes ever happened."

He walked over to my telephone and dropped the pen into my pencil mug.

"See?"

"Reid—"

"Please, Deborah. All I'm asking is that you wait about talking to Dwight. Give him a chance to find Lynn's real killer. Or—" He gave me a sharp, considering look. "Maybe we could find him first."

"We?"

"Why not? We're both professionals. Taking depositions is what we do. And people talk to civilians like us quicker than they'll talk to Dwight. We just ask a few questions around town, listen hard to all the gossip and figure it out. What do you say?"

His eager, almost adolescent expression suddenly reminded me of Mickey Rooney in those old movies Dwight and I sometimes watch.

I didn't feel one bit like Judy Garland though and I sure as hell didn't want to try putting on a show in the barn.

"How hard can it be for us to figure out who was balling her?" Reid wheedled, as he followed me out to the kitchen. "She didn't do it in the middle of Main Street or in her own house, even, but she sure wasn't the most discreet woman I ever slept with."

"Do you suppose Jason knew?" I asked, pouring us a cup of the freshly brewed coffee.

"Had to, you'd think." Reid reached into my refrigerator for milk and kept dribbling it in until his coffee was more *au lait* than *café*. "Unless he's one of those husbands who makes a point of not knowing? He's such a grind though, maybe not."

"Grind? He was playing ball Saturday."

"Grind," Reid said firmly. "He and Millard King. Birds of a feather. And not just because they humped the same woman."

"How's that?"

"Both of them are ambitious as hell and both of 'em have at least two reasons for everything they do. Like playing ball. That's an appropriate 'guy' activity. Makes you seem human. Puts you right out there to bond with your peer group. Good social contacts. Like the way you moved your membership over to First Baptist in Dobbs," he added shrewdly.

"See?" said the preacher, who's always been embarrassed by that cynical act.

The pragmatist shrugged.

"Before it's over, you're going to see King and Bullock both on a statewide ballot," said Reid. "Just remember that you heard it here first."

"Elective office?"

"Why else do you think King's so hot to marry one of the homeliest gals that ever wore lipstick? Because she's connected on both sides of her family to some political heavy hitters, that's why. And in this state, you still need a ladywife to do the whole white-glove bit. If Lynn Bullock threatened to make a scandal, she could've scared the little debutante off. Soured things with her daddy the Justice."

His venom surprised me. "What's Millard King ever done to you?"

"Nothing really. Just sometimes I get a shade tired of the deserving poor."

"Come again?"

"All these up-by-their-bootstrap people, who keep reminding you that you were born with a silver spoon in your mouth while they had to work for everything they got," he said scornfully. "As if you're worth shit because your parents and your grandparents could read and write, while they're the *true* yeoman nobility who really deserve it. And all the time they're sneering, they're out there busting their balls to have what they think you're born to. As if money's all it takes."

"Why, Reid Stephenson! You really *are* a snob."

"If not apologizing for who and what my parents

are and what they gave me makes me a snob, then guilty as charged," he said as his scowl dissolved into one of those roguish smiles. "But I'm not guilty of murder."

"You're the one without an alibi though."

I drained the last of my coffee and as he took my mug to pour me another cup of the rich dark brew, we mulled over the other men known to be in Lynn Bullock's life.

"She died between five-fifteen and eight, give or take a few minutes," I said. "Dwight and I got to the ball field around four-thirty. Jason Bullock was right behind me when she called at five and after the game, he went straight from the field to the pizza place with us. We even followed him back to Cotton Grove."

"He may be out of it," said Reid, "but what about Millard King?"

"He told Dwight that he was there jogging for at least an hour, but I didn't notice him till he was coming off the track around six o'clock. I suppose he could have cut through the trees and jogged over from the Orchid Motel. It's on this side of the bypass and less than a quarter-mile as the crow flies."

"Or the jogger jogs," said Reid, brightening up a bit.

"Courthouse gossip says that she was with Brandon Frazier for a while."

"Yeah, I heard that, too, but so what? Frazier doesn't have a wife or anybody special and he doesn't act like someone planning to run for political office."

"Frazier and King. Not much of a pool," I observed.

"And neither of them threatened to wring her

neck," Reid said glumly. "There has to be somebody else, somebody we haven't heard about yet."

"Maybe we're going at this the wrong way," I said. "Maybe it's not who she slept with, but who she didn't. Like Dr. Jeremy Potts."

"Who?"

So I told him about young Dr. Potts, who would have walked away from his marriage with no strings attached to his income had it not been for Lynn Bullock's shrewd advice to his wife and Jason Bullock's equally shrewd representation.

"Oh, yeah, I heard about that. A professional degree as marital property. Good thing I made Dotty settle out of court."

(Tough talk, but Dotty herself told me that Reid was voluntarily paying twenty percent of his income for young Tip's support.

("I'm socking it all away in mutual funds for his education," she'd said complacently.

(Like most hotshot real estate agents in this part of the state, Dotty's doing very well for herself these days.)

"Did you hear that she's getting married again?" Reid asked abruptly.

"Who? Felicia Potts?"

"Dotty."

Most of the time, Reid kept the torch he carried for his ex-wife well hidden under his Casanova cloak, but every once in a while, I caught a glimpse of it. She was the love of his life and he'd screwed it up by screwing around.

I reached out and squeezed his arm. "Maybe I'll call

Amy," I said, offering what comfort I could. "See if she's heard anything about Dr. Potts."

Against my better judgment and only because it would be his word against mine if this ever came to Dwight's attention, it seemed I had agreed to keep quiet about my pen for the time being.

And now, God help me, I was even volunteering to ask a few questions on my own. And yeah, part of it might be to help Reid, but part of my very nature is a basic need to find the truth and bring the facts to judgment.

My internal preacher was not fooled by such high-flown rationalizations.

"You'd risk your career for curiosity? Curiosity killed the cat."

"But no cat ever caught a rat without it," said the *pragmatist.*

CHAPTER 13

The people of the North might differ radically from the people of the South in many ways, but in the presence of such a dreadful visitation of nature, involving suffering and death, the brotherhood of man asserts itself and all things else are forgotten.

After Reid left, I watched the late news. The situation in Iraq might be occupying the rest of the country's TV screens, but here in central North Carolina, most of the newscast was given over to Hurricane Fran which seemed to be heading straight toward Wilmington. It was packing winds of 130 miles per hour and forecasters were saying it could push in a wall of water twenty feet high. The sheer size of the storm—more than five hundred miles across—guaranteed that we were going to feel its effects here in the Triangle.

All along the coast, people were nailing sheets of

plywood over their windows and getting their boats out of the water. Portland and Avery were congratulating themselves for bringing their boat back to Dobbs.

Skycams showed us thick lines of headlights heading inland through the rainy night as coastal residents from Myrtle Beach to Manteo sought higher ground. Channel 11's Miriam Thomas and Larry Stogner spoke of ordered evacuations in both South Carolina and Ocracoke, which is linked to the mainland only by ferries. New Hanover County had ordered a voluntary evacuation of all beach communities, including Wrightsville Beach where some of my Wilmington colleagues live; while Brunswick County was taking no chances. Evacuation was mandatory on all the barrier islands.

Reporter Greg Barnes showed motels filling up fast and shelters that were opening in schools and fire stations around Fayetteville to help handle the evacuees.

Even Don Ross, WTVD's color man, was unusually serious as he reported on local grocery stores that were already experiencing a run on batteries and canned goods. Eric Curry's camera panned over empty bread shelves and depleted milk cases.

I tried to call Kidd, but all I got was his answering machine.

It was nearly midnight but I wasn't a bit sleepy. Instead, I switched off the television and roamed around the house restlessly. I had candles and a stash of batteries for my radio, a half a loaf of bread and a fresh quart of milk. I should be okay, but the dire predictions left me uneasy.

The rain had finally stopped and I went out to put

all the porch and lawn chairs into my garage. The night should have been quiet except for frogs and crickets, yet male voices floated faintly on the soggy warm air and sirens seemed to be converging from different directions. I was about to get my car out and go see what was happening, when headlights appeared on the lane that runs from Andrew's house to mine and connects with a homemade bridge across Possum Creek.

The truck slowed to a stop as it drew near me and I saw Andrew behind the wheel with his son, A.K. Just topping the rise a few yards behind was Robert on the farm's biggest tractor.

I ran over to meet them. "What's happening?"

"Rescue squad's been called out," said Andrew. "A car's gone in the creek and they want us to help get it out."

"Oh, no!" Without being invited, I ran around to the passenger side, pulled open the door and shoved in next to A.K.

"You know who it is?" he asked as his dad put it in gear for the creek. The tractor lights behind us lit up the cab.

"I hope not," I answered. "But you know Ralph Freeman, the preacher at Balm of Gilead? His wife was out this way today visiting one of their church members and she never came home."

"That don't sound good," said Andrew. "No, sir, that don't sound good at all."

We came out onto the hardtop just south of the creek, where it bends at the bridge before the turn-in to the homeplace.

The curve was lit up like a carnival. Flashing lights of red, yellow, and blue bounced against the low-lying clouds and were reflected back in ghastly hues. Three patrol cars, a fire truck, and a rescue truck had their spotlights aimed down toward the muddy water that rushed under the bridge. The creek had flooded its channel and was as high as I'd ever seen it.

Men were out there in it up to their necks, working around the door of a white car whose top projected only a few inches above the turbulent waters. I recognized Donny Turner and Rudy Peacock from the West Colleton volunteer fire department—both were too big to miss—and skinny little Skeeter Collins from the Cotton Grove rescue squad. Five or six other dark and indistinguishable figures milled around in the water and I heard someone yell, "Damn! Is that a cottonmouth?"

"Fuck the cottonmouth and hand me the damn collar!" cried Skeeter.

By the glare of the spotlights, I saw the men relay a cervical collar to him without letting the water touch it. Skeeter's head disappeared inside the car.

"That's a good sign, ain't—*isn't* it?" asked A.K. "They don't put collars on dead people, do they?"

"I don't know," I said, wondering how they could possibly remove Clara Freeman—if it *was* Clara Freeman—from the car without drowning her in the process.

"Watch it, boys!" Skeeter shouted. "I felt it start to shift."

"Get that tractor in here," said the fire chief. "We need to get a chain or something on this car."

Robert backed his big John Deere down through

the bushes at the water's edge. There was a winch above the drawbar and someone grabbed the hook and waded into the water with it. Robert let the cable feed out slowly as the man hauled the hook over toward the car where other hands reached for it. There was a confused splashing around the end of the car and several strangled coughs as men came up gasping for air before the hook was securely attached to the back undercarriage.

There were also enough strangled curses to make me glad I was a woman on the shore instead of a man out there in the middle of a muddy, moccasin-infested creek. (We may be technically equal these days but that doesn't mean we jump into every activity with equal enthusiasm.)

Finally, a vaguely familiar voice called, "Put some tension on it, but for God's sake, go easy!"

That's when I recognized that the man who'd carried the hook out to the car was Jason Bullock. I'd heard that he'd joined a lot of civic organizations like the volunteer fire department, but this was the first time I'd seen him since the night of our post-game pizza over in Dobbs.

With the tractor in its lowest gear and half a dozen men doing what they could to support the car upright, Robert kept the cable taut as he slowly pulled until the Honda was on solid ground. Water was still waist-high where the men now stood on what was normally the creekbank, but at least there was no immediate danger of losing the car and the person inside. A lightweight molded plastic stretcher board was passed from the rescue truck and soon they had a recumbent form strapped onto it.

When they came ashore, I saw that it was indeed Clara Freeman, unconscious and with all her vital signs erratic, but alive.

Dwight had arrived by then. As they loaded Mrs. Freeman into the ambulance, he turned to me with a lopsided smile. "Sometimes I'm glad I listen to you. If she'd spent the night out there . . ."

"Another two inches and her nose would have been in the water," said a dripping Jason Bullock as we watched the ambulance speed away with lights flashing and siren wailing. "Anybody call her husband yet? He ought to be told."

My heart went out to him in his empathy for Ralph Freeman and I knew he was probably remembering his own tense hours of worry before Dwight came and told him the worst a husband can hear.

"The dispatcher's calling him right now," Dwight said. "She'll tell him to meet the ambulance at Dobbs Memorial."

I put out my hand to Jason and told him how sorry I was for his own loss. He thanked me, then looked at Dwight. "I've tried not to bug you, Bryant, but do you have anything yet?"

"Sorry. We have a few leads, but nothing solid. But maybe you could come by the office tomorrow and let's talk again? Go over a few possibilities?"

"Sure."

We stood there on the side of the road and watched as the excitement wound down and the volunteers packed it in. The fire truck trundled across the bridge, back toward Cotton Grove, the extra patrol cars headed off to their usual sectors, and the remaining deputy showed Dwight the sketch he'd made to explain how Clara Freeman wound up in Possum Creek.

"We'll check again tomorrow in the daylight, but we couldn't see skid marks. Looks like she came flying down the slope, misjudged the curve and drove straight off the road without touching the brakes, going so fast, she just sailed into the creek."

I was craning over Dwight's shoulder, but Jason stared back up the slope that was now washed in light by Robert's tractor lights.

"You reckon she might've blacked out? Or the gas pedal stuck?"

"With a stuck accelerator, she'd have been standing on her brakes," said Dwight.

"And if she was blacked out," said the deputy, "she wouldn't've been going fast enough to skip the bank."

"Hey, Deb'rah," Andrew called. "You ready to go?"

It was getting late and he had a couple of bulk barns loaded with curing tobacco to see to.

"Go on ahead," I called back. "I'll ride with Robert."

All this time, local traffic had come and gone sporadically on this back road. When we first arrived, it was one-lane, directed by a trooper who kept the rubberneckers moving. This late, long past midnight, in a community that was still mostly farmers and early-rising blue-collar workers, the road was practically deserted. Nevertheless, an occasional car came by and slowed to ask whether everything was under control. If they knew Dwight or recognized Robert's tractor, the driver would even get out of his vehicle and come over to gawk at Clara Freeman's drowned car.

My brother Robert had finished pulling it up onto

the shoulder of the road and water streamed from the open doors. I walked over to have a look myself while Dwight and his deputy finished conferring and Jason was right behind me when an oncoming car slowed, stopped, and a man came toward us.

"Evening, Judge," said Millard King. "That's not your car, is it? You all right?"

I sensed Jason Bullock stiffening behind me and I knew that King hadn't immediately realized who was standing there with me. In the half-light cast by reflected headlights, I saw recognition spread across his face when he came closer.

"Bullock." His voice was neutral as he nodded to Jason.

"King." Jason's voice was equally neutral, but I finally had an answer to whether or not he knew his wife had been sleeping around.

And with whom.

Like a nervous hostess smoothing over an awkward social lapse, I found myself chattering about the accident, about Jason's part in helping to rescue Clara Freeman and how lucky she was to have been found before drowning.

"You live around here?" Jason Bullock asked bluntly.

Now that he mentioned it, what *was* Millard King doing on this back road at this hour?

"Just down in Makely," he answered easily. "But my brother lives over in Fuquay, so I'm up and down this road a lot. You say she went in this afternoon sometime? I sure didn't notice when I came through around eight. 'Course, it was still raining then."

"Oh look!" I said. "There's Lashanda's baby doll."

188

I went over and pulled a soggy brown rubber doll from the car. As I did, I saw something lumpy on the floor beneath the steering wheel. Clara Freeman's pocketbook. I gathered it up, too, thinking that I'd carry it to the hospital with me tomorrow morning.

The two men circled the car.

"It's amazing," said King. "The car doesn't seem to have a scratch on it."

"Dry it out and it should be good as new," agreed Bullock.

My brother Robert came over, put the car in neutral and closed the doors. "What you planning to do with the car, Dwight? Want me to tow it over to Jimmy White's garage?"

"Would you mind?"

"Naw, but he ain't gonna be up this time of night."

"That's okay. I'll call him first thing tomorrow."

As I climbed up to the glassed-in cab of the big tractor with Robert, I saw King and Bullock walk to their separate cars. I guess they didn't have much to say to each other.

Not tonight anyhow.

Jimmy's garage was only a couple of miles away and the car pulled easily, so we were there in ten minutes. Not surprisingly, the building was dark and silent, as was Jimmy's house out back, behind a thick row of Leland cypresses.

I helped Robert unhitch the car. We left the key in the ignition switch, although I did detach it from Clara's keyring. When we climbed back into the tractor cab, I stuck the keyring in Clara's soggy handbag and tucked it back under the tractor seat so I could hold on.

Now that we weren't towing the car, Robert put it in gear and soon we were jouncing briskly across rutted dirt lanes. The tractor is air-conditioned and has an AM/FM radio, but Robert keeps the tape deck loaded with Patsy, Hank and George.

"Ain't no country music on the radio no more," he said. "Hell of a note when country stations don't play nothing but Garth Brooks and Dixie Chicks and think that's country."

We rode through the night harmonizing along with Ernest Tubbs and Loretta Lynn on "Sweet Thang," a song that used to really crack me up when I was six.

CHAPTER 14

"Prepare for the worst, which is yet to come," were the only consoling words of the weather bureau officials.

The calls started at daybreak.

"You got you plenty of batteries laid in?" asked Robert.

"Batteries?" I asked groggily.

"They're saying we're definitely gonna get us some of that hurricane. You want to make sure your flashlight works when the lights go off."

"We got an extra kerosene lantern," said his wife Doris, who was on their extension phone. "How 'bout I send Robert over with it?"

Less than ninety seconds after they rang off, it was Haywood and Isabel.

"Don't forget to bring in all your porch chairs," said Haywood.

191

"And fill some milk jugs with clean water," said Isabel.

"Water?" I yawned.

"If the power goes, so does your water pump."

Seth and Minnie were also solicitous of my water supply.

"I've already got both bathtubs filled," Minnie said. "This hot weather, you want to be able to flush if the electricity goes out."

I hadn't lost power since I moved into my new house the end of July, but it wasn't unusual when I was growing up out here in the country. It seldom stayed off more than a couple of days and since we heated with woodstoves that could double as cookstoves, no electricity wasn't much of a hardship in the winter. More like going camping in your house. Especially since it was usually caused by an ice storm that had closed school anyhow, so that you got to stay home and go sliding during the day, then come in to hot chocolate and a warm and cozy candlelit evening of talking or making music around the stove.

Summer was a little worse. We never had air-conditioning so we didn't expect to stay cool even when the electricity was on, but running out of ice for our tea and soft drinks was a problem. And two days were about as long as you could trust food from the refrigerator in hot weather.

I emptied the ice bin into a plastic bag so that my icemaker would make a fresh batch. And I dutifully filled my tub, kettle, and a couple of pots with water since I had no empty plastic jugs on hand.

Daddy drove through the yard with my newspaper

and said I ought to come over and stay at the home-place till the hurricane had passed.

I pointed out that my new house had steel framing and was guaranteed to hold up under winds of a hundred and seventy miles an hour, "So maybe you should spend the night with me."

"Mine's stood solid through a hundred years of storms and Hazel, too, and it ain't never even lost a piece of tin." The mention of tin must have reminded him of the house trailer Herman's son Reese was renting from Seth because he added, "Reese is gonna come. And Maidie and Cletus."

Now a hurricane party was a tempting thought and I told him I'd let him know.

After he left and before someone else could tie up my line, I picked up the phone to call Kidd even though he was probably already gone. And then I put it back down again, more than a little annoyed. After all, shouldn't he be worried about me? The way Fran was lining up, Colleton County was just as likely to get hit as New Bern. Couldn't he find a spare minute to see if I was okay?

No?

Then he could damn well wonder.

With all the distractions, I was halfway to Dobbs before I remembered Clara Freeman's purse and Lashanda's doll. No time to go back for them if I wanted to check past the hospital before going to court.

At Dobbs Memorial, it was only a few minutes past eight but the intensive care unit's waiting room was jammed with Balm of Gilead members. A couple of

Ralph Freeman's colleagues from the middle school where he taught were there, along with some ministers from nearby churches. I greeted those I recognized and learned that Clara Freeman was in critical but stable condition. They had operated on her early this morning to relieve the pressure on her brain but it was too soon to make predictions, although Ralph was with the surgeon now.

Mingled with the hospital smells of antiseptics and floor wax were the appetizing aromas of hot coffee and fast-food breakfast meals—sausage biscuits from Hardee's, Egg McMuffins, and Krispy Kreme doughnuts—nourishment for people who'd evidently been here since Mrs. Freeman was brought in last night.

Stan and his little sister were seated against the far wall and I went over to them.

"Stan, Lashanda, I'm so sorry about your mother."

"Thank you, Miss Deborah," the boy said.

Before he could say anything else, the large elderly man who sat beside him said, "Stanley, will you introduce this lady to me?"

It may have been couched as a request, but the tone sounded awfully like an order to me.

"Yes, sir. This is Judge Deborah Knott," he said with touching formality. "Miss Deborah, this is my grandfather, the Reverend James McElroy Gaithers."

"Judge?" He looked faintly disapproving. Because I was a judge? (*"I suffer not a woman to teach, nor to usurp authority over the man."*) Or because I was white? (*"He shall separate them one from another."*)

"Yes, sir," I said. "District Court. And you're Mrs. Freeman's father?"

"I am."

There are many preachers who prefer the Old Testament to the New and the Reverend James McElroy Gaithers was clearly one of them. For him, I was pretty sure that the dominant element of the Trinity would be God the stern father of retribution, not Jesus the forgiving son.

"You're from Warrenton, I believe?"

He nodded magisterially.

"It's a sad thing that brings you down here," I commiserated. "I'm really sorry."

"My daughter is in the hands of the Lord," he said. "His will shall be done."

At the old man's words, Stan looked stricken and little Lashanda simply looked miserable. Was there no one to rescue the children from this Jeremiah and give them true comfort? Where was Clara Freeman's good friend that Ralph had mentioned last night? Rosa Somebody? Surely she was somewhere in this crowd and with a hint dropped into her ear, maybe she would—

Stan's face suddenly brightened at the sight of someone behind me and I turned to see Cyl DeGraffenried.

I had to hand it to her. For a woman who was falling apart the last time I saw her, she was in complete control now, poised and professional in a crisp hunter green linen suit with soft white silk blouse and matching low-heeled pumps. Her hair fell in artful perfection around her lovely face and pearls gleamed coolly at her throat and earlobes.

She spoke to Stan and Lashanda, was introduced to their grandfather, immediately sized up the situation and said to him in solicitous female tones, "I know you'll want to speak privately with the doctor when he comes, so why don't the Judge and I take your grandchildren out for some fresh air and breakfast?"

Both children immediately stood up as Cyl looked at me brightly. "Deborah?"

"Sure," I said, trying not to look as taken aback as I actually was.

My court session was technically due to start at nine, but by the time most ADAs finish working out their plea bargains and stipulations, things seldom get moving much before nine-thirty or a quarter till ten, so we had more than an hour to give the children.

Reverend Gaithers started to object but Cyl blithely chose to misunderstand him. "No, no, you do *not* have to thank us. It's no trouble at all. We haven't had breakfast yet either, have we, Deborah?"

We made our getaway through the swinging doors and came face-to-face with Ralph Freeman and a doctor in surgical scrubs.

Ralph looked at us in confusion and Cyl seemed suddenly out of words herself.

"Daddy!" cried Lashanda and bounded into his arms.

"Is Mama going to be all right?" asked Stan.

"Dr. Potts thinks so," Ralph said, swinging his daughter up to hug her as he nodded toward his companion.

Having only seen a man in a suit and tie when I was deciding on his divorce settlement, I hadn't immediately recognized Dr. Jeremy Potts. He knew me though, and gave a sour tilt of the head.

"We were just coming in so Dr. Potts can explain to Clara's father." He kissed Lashanda and stood her back on her own feet. "Thanks, Deborah, for getting extra patrol cars out to look for her. Somebody said you helped pull her out?"

The children stared at me, wide-eyed.

"Not me, my brother Robert. His tractor. With a lot of help from the fire and rescue squads. I just did the heavy looking on." I smiled down at Lashanda. "I saved your doll though. Oh, and your wife's purse and keys," I told Ralph. "I forgot to bring them in with me, but I'll get them to you as soon as I can."

"No hurry," he said. "I'm afraid she's not going to be driving any time soon."

He was now under control enough to speak directly to Cyl. "Where are y'all off to?"

Stan spoke up. "Miss Cyl and Miss Deborah's taking us out to breakfast."

"If that's okay with you?" Cyl managed to add. "We thought they could use a break from the waiting room."

"That's very kind of y'all."

He looked at her as if he didn't want to stop looking and my heart broke for them, but Dr. Potts cleared his throat and said, "Mr. Freeman?"

"Sorry, Doctor. I guess I'm holding you up."

The two men went on into the waiting room and we drove over to the north end of Main Street in Cyl's car. The air was thick with humidity and the sky was full of low gray clouds. There wasn't much wind here on the ground, but overhead, those clouds scudded eerily past like frantic dirty sheep scattering before wolves we couldn't yet see.

*   *   *

197

The Coffee Pot has a long counter where hungry folks in a hurry perch, a big round table with ashtrays for retirees who are more interested in gossip than food, and four non-smoking booths in back for those who want a little privacy.

We took a booth and Ava Dupree came straight over with a menu, her pale blue eyes bright with curiosity. My brother Herman's electrical shop is right next door and we often meet here for coffee. Ava greeted Cyl by name, too, but she didn't recognize the children and she's not shy about asking personal questions.

"Freeman? Oh, yeah, your mama's the one that went and run off the road into Possum Creek last night, ain't she? I heard 'em talking about it first thing this morning. She's gonna be okay, ain't she?"

"We sure could use some orange juice here, Ava," I said pointedly.

"And how about some blueberry pancakes, bacon, milk and coffee?" said Cyl. "That okay with y'all?"

Next to me, Stan nodded agreement and Lashanda, seated beside Cyl, smiled shyly. Blue barrettes in the shape of little bluebirds were clipped to the ends of all her braids.

Stan knew Cyl because she'd given him a lift home from my Fourth of July pig-picking last month and from seeing her at the ball field, but she was a stranger to the little girl.

Not for long though.

"Somebody just lost a tooth," Cyl said. "Was the Tooth Fairy good to you?"

"I thought she wasn't," the child replied, " 'cause guess what? My tooth was still in the glass this morning when I woke up! But Stan said it was because too many people were in the house awake last night and maybe she got afraid."

"Shandy!" An awkward, bony preadolescent, eleven-year-old Stan looked so exceedingly self-conscious that I could almost swear he was blushing, but his little sister was oblivious.

"And guess what? When I came back from brushing my teeth, my tooth was gone and guess what was in the water?"

She drew her hand out of her pocket and proudly showed us two shiny quarters.

"Hey, that's really cool," Cyl said, smiling at Stan. "She never left me more than a dime."

"Inflation." Stan grinned.

By the time our pancakes arrived, she had charmed them both. Stan told us about a school science project he was working on—how he'd been documenting Fran's path from the time she was nothing more than a tropical depression off the coast of Africa till whatever happened in the next twenty-four hours. I learned things about hurricanes I'd never given much thought to before.

"They're saying it's going to be one of the really big ones!" He gestured so excitedly as he described the spiraling bands of storms around the eye that the plastic syrup dispenser went flying and he had to get up and chase it down.

Lashanda looked less than thrilled by the approaching storm and moved closer to Cyl till she was tucked up almost under Cyl's arm. "I wish we could spend the night at your house."

Cyl put her arm around the child and gave a little squeeze. "I wish you could, too, baby."

"Shandy!" said her brother.

"Grandfather scares me." A tear slid down her cheek. "And Mama's not coming home tonight and if Daddy stays with her and we get tornadoes—"

Her lip quivered.

"What about your mother's friend?" I asked. "Someone named Rosa?"

"Miss Rosa hasn't come yet," said Stan. "She must've worked last night 'cause we couldn't get her on the phone either."

Not much of a best friend, I thought, thinking how I'd react if something like this happened to Portland or Morgan or Dixie or two or three other close friends.

"And you just might have just a little more freedom to come and go when you like," the preacher reminded me. "You don't know what obstacles of job or children might be keeping her away."

"Don't worry," Cyl told Lashanda. "Things will work out."

She wet a napkin in a glass of water and gently wiped the little girl's sticky lips.

When we delivered the children back to the ICU waiting room, Ralph immediately came over and thanked us again.

"How is Mrs. Freeman really?" Cyl asked when Stan and Lashanda spotted friends of their own age and moved away from us.

"Really?" Ralph shook his head, clearly weary from lack of sleep and a deep sadness. "Dr. Potts can't say. She should have regained consciousness by now, but she hasn't. There are broken ribs, bruised windpipe from the seat belt—thank God she was wearing it! Those things are relatively superficial. But the concussion . . . and of course, the longer she's in a coma, the worse the prospects. Maybe by lunchtime we'll know better."

The mention of lunchtime made me look at my watch. Ten after nine.

I squeezed Ralph's hand. "We have to go now, but we'll be praying for her."

"You'll come back?"

"Yes," said Cyl.

She was silent in the elevator down and as we walked out through the parking lot, I said, "You okay?"

"I'm holding it together." She gave me an unhappy smile. "For the moment anyhow."

"See you at the courthouse, then." I headed for my car a few spaces past hers, then stopped short. "Oh, damn!"

"What?" asked Cyl.

"Somebody's popped the lock on my trunk again." I was totally exasperated. This was the second time in a year. "What the hell do they think I carry?"

"They take anything?" she asked, peering over my shoulder.

My briefcase was still there. So were my robe and the heavy locked toolbox where I stash wrenches, screwdrivers, pliers, extra windshield wipers and the registered .38 Daddy gave me when I told him I was going to keep on driving deserted roads at night and that I didn't need a man to protect me. Things had been stirred and the roll of paper towels was tangled in my robe, but I couldn't see that anything was missing.

I transferred robe and briefcase to the front seat and wired the trunk lid down. It irked me that I was going to have to spend my morning break filing another police complaint so I could prove to the insurance company that the damage really happened.

Court was disjointed that morning, complicated by a bunch of no-shows and motions to recalendar due to the weather. With Fran expected to come ashore tonight somewhere between Myrtle Beach and Wilmington, everyone seemed to have trouble concentrating and by the time I gave up and adjourned for the day at one p.m., the wind had picked up and it was raining hard again.

Frankly, I was getting more than a little tired of both the anticipation and the rain, too.

"Enough already!" I grumbled to Luther Parker, with whom I share a connecting bathroom. "Let's just have a good blow and get it over with and get back to sunshine."

"Hope it's that easy," he said.

Everything smelled musty and felt damp. I almost slipped off my shoes and wiggled my stockinged toes just to make sure they weren't starting to grow little webs.

At the midmorning break, when I reported my jimmied trunk to the Dobbs town police, I'd cut through the Sheriff's Department to gripe about it to Dwight, but his office was empty.

He was there at one-fifteen, though, munching a hamburger at his desk. I started through the door of his office singing my song of woe, then stopped when I saw Terry Wilson sitting at the other end of the desk with his own hamburger and drink can.

"What's happened, Terry?" There's only a short list of things to bring an SBI agent out during working hours. "Dwight? Somebody get killed?"

"Yeah. One of the maids out at the Orchid Motel," Dwight said. "Lived in Cotton Grove. A neighbor found her around five this morning. Somebody sliced her up pretty bad last night. Knocked her around first, then cut off one of her fingers slick as a surgeon would. While she was still alive. Blood everywhere."

I watched as Terry squirted a tinfoil packet of ketchup on his french fries. I guess you get anesthetized after a while.

"Is her death related to Lynn Bullock's?"

"Be a right big coincidence if it isn't," said Terry, who's as tolerant of my questions as Dwight.

"You get any hint of it when you interviewed her?" I asked Dwight.

"The thing is, we never did," he admitted with a huge sigh of regret. "She got off work before the Bullock woman checked in and didn't come back on duty till the next day, long after the killing took place. Didn't seem to be any urgency about talking with her. Sloppy."

"Don't beat up on yourself," said Terry, as I opened Dwight's little refrigerator and helped myself to one of the cold drinks inside. "You and your people were all over that motel. If Rosa Edwards knew something about the murder, she should've—"

"Rosa Edwards?" I asked, popping the top of a Diet Pepsi. "That's who got killed?"

"Yeah," said Dwight. "You know her?"

I shook my head. "No, but Ralph Freeman said she was his wife's closest friend here." I stared at them, struck by a sudden thought. "What if it's nothing to do with Lynn Bullock? What if it's about how Clara Freeman wound up in Possum Creek without leaving any skid marks on the pavement?"

Dwight reached for his Rolodex and started dialing. "Jimmy? You done anything yet with that Honda Civic Robert Knott pulled out of the creek last night? . . . Good. Don't touch it. I'm sending a crew out to examine it."

CHAPTER 15

But when their hearts are really touched
they drop everything and rush to the rescue of the afflicted.

Cyl stuck her head in my office as I was sliding my
feet into a pair of sandals so old that it wouldn't matter if they got soaked. I saw that she, too, had changed
from those expensive dark green heels to scuffed black
flats that had seen better days. Fran was still out in the
Atlantic, just off the coast of Wilmington, but so huge
that her leading edge was already spilling into the Triangle area. We were in for a night of high wind and
heavy rain whether or not the hurricane actually came
inland.

Cyl had heard about Rosa Edwards's murder, but
she hadn't connected it to Clara Freeman until I told
her of their friendship. Instantly, her thoughts flew to
Stan and Lashanda. Their mother was in a coma, her

closest friend had been brutally butchered and a big storm was on the way. Anything that touched Ralph Freeman was going to touch her but she did seem genuinely distressed for the children, who might have to stay alone with their stern-faced grandfather.

"I could take them to my grandmother's, but she's already gone to my uncle's house in Durham."

"I'm sure some kind family from the church will take them in," I soothed.

I was anxious to head back to the farm, but Cyl asked if I'd go with her to the hospital and I couldn't turn her down since it was only the second time she'd ever asked me for a favor.

The sky was dark as we drove in tandem to the hospital on the northwest side of Dobbs and the ICU waiting room was nearly empty except for the children, the Reverend James McElroy Gaithers, and a couple of church people who were clearly torn between a wish to comfort and an even more sincere wish to get home under shelter before the wind got too heavy.

Lashanda was sitting on Ralph's lap and her eyes lit up as we came through the door. Heaven help him, so did Ralph's. His father-in-law gave a stately nod that acknowledged our acquaintance.

"You sure you kids don't want to come home with Crystal and me?" I heard one of the women coax as we joined them.

Lashanda sank deeper into her father's arms and Ralph said, "Thank you, Sister Garrett, but they'll be fine here. I already spoke to one of the staff about some blankets and pillows. They can stretch out here on the couches."

Impulsively, I excused myself and went and found a telephone.

Daddy doesn't like talking on the phone and he answered with his usual abrupt, "Yeah?"

I quickly explained the situation.

"Bring 'em on here," he said, before I could ask. "I'll tell Maidie. And, Deb'rah?"

"Sir?"

"Don't y'all dilly-dally around. They's gonna be tree limbs down in the road 'fore long, so come on now, you hear?"

I heard.

When I got back, Cyl was extending her own invitation to the children.

"I've got a better idea," I told her brightly. "My daddy just invited you and Stan and Lashanda to his hurricane party."

"Hurricane party?" asked Lashanda. The bluebird barrettes on her braids brushed her cheeks as she uncurled a bit from Ralph's protective arms. "What's that?"

"That's where we have like a pajama party and while the wind's blowing and the rain's coming down, we're snug inside with candles and lanterns. We'll sit up half the night, make popcorn and sing and tell stories—"

The Reverend Gaithers cleared his throat.

"—but mostly we'll just laugh at any old storm that tries to scare us," I finished hastily. "And Stan can take notes for his science project and tell us what's happening."

"Can we, Daddy?"

For the first time since we'd come back, the little

girl seemed animated instead of tired and apprehensive. Even Stan looked interested.

"Please?" I appealed to Ralph. "You've been out to the farm. It's not all that far from Cotton Grove so you could easily swing by if you should go home tomorrow morning."

"We-ell," said Ralph. "You sure it's not too much trouble."

"No trouble at all," I assured him. "There's plenty of room for you, too, Reverend Gaithers, if you'd care to come," I added.

"Thank you," he said gravely, "but I will keep the vigil for my daughter here."

The brightness faded from Stan's face. "I guess I better stay, too."

"No," said the older man, showing more compassion than I'd credited him with. "You go and look after your sister, Stanley. Your father and I will do the praying tonight."

"You'll come, too, Miss Cyl?" Stan asked as Lashanda slid off Ralph's lap and took Cyl's hand.

Confused, Cyl started to murmur about not having the right clothes, but I quickly scotched that. "I have everything you need, even an extra toothbrush. Come on. It'll be fun."

She might have hesitated longer, but one of Bo Poole's deputies, Mayleen Richards, entered the waiting room and we both knew that she'd probably come to question Ralph about Rosa Edwards's death. The children didn't seem to know about it yet and Cyl and I were in instant silent agreement that this was no time to hit them with another shock.

"Sure," said Cyl. "Let's go."

Downstairs, we agreed to split up. Cyl would drive Stan and Lashanda to Cotton Grove for their overnight things while I stopped by Jimmy White's to see what he could do about my trunk lock, then we'd meet at the homeplace. Maidie was active in the same church as Cyl's grandmother, so Cyl would see at least one familiar face if they got there before I did.

Even though it wasn't yet three o'clock, the road home was busier than usual. A lot of places must have let their employees go home early. Rain was falling quite heavily now and wind gusts buffeted my car, giving me pleasant little bursts of adrenaline each time I had to correct the steering. It was both scary and exhilarating. Like riding a horse you're not too sure of.

When I reached Jimmy's garage and pulled into his drive, the county's crime scene van blocked the entrance to the garage itself and Dwight's car was there, too.

They had pushed Clara Freeman's Civic inside and found what we hadn't noticed the night before: a small dent in her left rear fender and a smear of black paint ground into that dent. It might just be enough.

"*If* we can find a black car to match it with," Dwight said with unwonted pessimism. "And you want to hear something cute? I stopped by the Orchid Motel on my way out of Dobbs and Marie O'Day said she was just about to call me. They'd heard about Edwards's death and one of the maids finally thought to mention that she came back to the motel late Saturday afternoon. Guess what car she was driving?"

"This one here?"

"You got it," he said glumly. "Rosa Edwards might still be alive if we'd talked to her."

"Or not," I said, patting his shoulder as if he were Reese or A.K. "If she was the talking kind, she had four days to come to you."

It would have been interesting to bat around theories, but we all were getting antsy. Jimmy promised to get to my trunk lock by the first of the week, but right now he wanted to close down the garage. Dwight had a few loose ends of his own to see to before the storm got worse. The crime scene van was already on its way back to Dobbs.

I hurried on home to change clothes and pick up some overnight things for Cyl and me. As I was hunting for the extra toothbrushes I'd stashed in my linen closet, Robert stopped by with a kerosene lantern, Lashanda's doll and Clara Freeman's purse, which were still soggy and starting to mildew after such a hot day in the airless cab of his tractor. I gave him a hug for the lantern and thanks for remembering the doll and purse.

"I'm real glad you and Reese're going to Daddy's," he said, hugging me back. "It's not gonna be anything like Hazel, but it don't pay to take risks."

I tried to stick up for my house's steel framing, but he just laughed and drove on off toward his own place.

I took the things inside and put them on my kitchen counter. The mildew wiped right off Lashanda's rubber doll and Clara's brown plastic purse. I rinsed out the doll's dress and underpants and threw them in the dryer. Next, I unloaded the purse and propped it open, then spread the contents across the countertop so they'd dry and air out—keys, lipstick, comb, nail file, a damp notepad with a list of items crossed off, a couple of envelopes. One was plain and sealed with Scotch tape. The other looked like a bill from Carolina Power and Light. I threw away a couple of sodden tissues and a half-melted roll of breath mints.

Along with the usual cards and paper money in the wallet, there were pictures of Stan and Lashanda and a studio picture of Clara and Ralph with the two kids. I looked at that one long and hard. In her neat blue dress with a chaste white collar, she was no-where near as beautiful as Cyl, but there was some-thing wistful in her eyes and I wondered if Ralph had been unfaithful to her before or was Cyl an aberration waiting to happen? I tried to imagine Cyl into this picture if Clara didn't make it. Cyl as a preacher's wife? As stepmother to these two chil-dren? Cyl DeGraffenried of the sophisticated hair-cut, the elegant understated clothes, the competitive career woman?

There'd be a lot of hard adjusting all around.

I put down paper towels and spread the pictures and cards to dry as I switched on the radio. Bulletins were coming thick and fast on WPTF. Fran was definitely coming ashore around eight o'clock at Bald Head Is-land at the mouth of the Cape Fear River.

Rain was falling hard in long windblown sheets that almost obscured the pond as it lashed at my windows. I went around making a final check and had just latched the last window when the phone rang.

"Your people are here," said Daddy. "Why ain't you?"

"On my way," I told him and dashed out into the rain with my duffle bag crammed with enough clothes and toiletries to last a week.

CHAPTER 16

Here are all the terrible phenomena of the
West Indian hurricane—the tremendous
wind, the thrashing sea, the lightning, the
bellowing thunder, and the drowning rain
that seems to be dashed from mighty
tanks with the force of Titans.

We spent the next hour settling in. Since the quick-
est way to get people past their initial awkwardness is
to give them something to do, Maidie and I soon had
Lashanda and Stan racing up and down the stairs,
bringing down pillows, quilts and blankets. Here at
the homeplace, kitchen and den flow into each other
and Daddy and Cletus sat at the kitchen table to keep
from getting run over.

There were enough bedrooms in this old house for
everyone to have a choice, but who ever heard of
going off to separate rooms during a hurricane party?

The den couch opens into a bed that I claimed for

Cyl and me, and there were a couple of recliner chairs as well. We made thick pallets for the children right on the area rugs that dot the worn linoleum floor.

Both Blue and Ladybelle had been turned in and Ladybelle immediately went over and started pushing at Lashanda's hand with her head.

"She wants you to scratch behind her ears," Daddy told her.

Half-apprehensively—the hound was almost as tall as she was—Lashanda reached out and scratched. Ladybelle gave a sigh of pure pleasure and sank down at the little girl's feet.

Daddy's television was tuned to the weather channel and Stan sat on the floor in front of it, entranced by the colored graphics that covered the screen.

"So *that's* what he looks like," he murmured when a black forecaster started explaining for the umpteenth time how the Saffir-Simpson scale rated hurricanes. "I wondered."

"You don't have cable?" Cyl asked, stuffing pillows into cotton pillowcases that Maidie had ironed to crisp perfection.

"We don't have television at all," said Lashanda, abandoning Ladybelle so that she could help Cyl.

Stan looked embarrassed. "Mama doesn't believe in it. But I can pick up this channel on my shortwave. That's how I know that guy's voice."

I wasn't as shocked as some people might be. Like a lot of members in her fundamentalist church, my sister-in-law Nadine doesn't, quote, believe in television either, but Herman's overruled her on that from the beginning. And as soon as cable came to Dobbs, he signed up for it. Now that the population's getting dense enough to make it economically feasible, cable's finally reached our end of the county, too, but Daddy and the boys have had satellite dishes for years.

All the same, even though I could understand where Clara Freeman was coming from—especially after meeting her father—it did make me wonder how much slack she cut her children.

Or her husband.

"They's crayons in the children's drawer," Maidie reminded me on one of her trips through the den, when she realized Stan was trying to copy some of the color graphics of the storm.

The television sat atop an enormous old turn-of-the-century sideboard. Mother had turned the bottom drawer into a catchall for games and toys as soon as the first grandchild was born. And yes, it was now being used for great-grandchildren, so it still held a big Tupperware bowl full of broken crayons of all colors. Some of them had probably been there since Reese was a baby. Stan seized upon them and one of his blank weather maps soon sported an amorphous gray storm with a dark red blotch in the center.

All this time, the house had been filling with delicious aromas. For Maidie, picnics and parties always mean fried chicken and she had the meaty parts of at least four chickens bubbling away in three large black iron frying pans. There was a bowl of potato salad in the refrigerator, a big pot of newly picked butter beans on the spare burner, and Maidie set Cletus to slicing a half-dozen fresh-off-the-vine tomatoes while she got out her bread tray.

"You've already cooked enough for an army," I said

as Cyl and Lashanda and I set the table. "Don't tell me you're going to make biscuits, too?"

"Well, you know how Reese eats." She was already mixing shortening into a mound of self-rising flour. "And that Stan looks like he could stand some fattening."

Lashanda giggled, her little blue barrettes jiggling with each movement. "And you know what? Mama says he eats like he's got a tapeworm."

I had to smile, too. You don't grow up in a houseful of adolescent boys without hearing that phrase a time or twenty.

Following his nose, Reese blew in through the back door a few minutes later, carrying a full ice chest as if it weighed no more than a five-pound bag of sugar. Like his father Herman, Reese is also a twin, but he's built like all the other Knott men: six feet tall, sandy brown hair, clear blue eyes. No movie stars in the whole lot, but no trouble getting women either.

"Something sure smells fit to eat in this house," he said, buttering Maidie before he was even through the door good.

He spotted Cyl and Lashanda, did a double take and then squatted down so he'd be level with the child. "Well, well, well! Who's this pretty little thing we got here?"

His words were for Lashanda, but his eyes were all over Cyl, who had changed into the jeans and T-shirt I'd brought her. Both were a trifle snug on me, but she had room to spare in all the right places.

"Behave yourself, Reese," I scolded and introduced him to our guests.

"Oh, yeah, Uncle Robert told me about Miz Freeman. I'm real sorry." He straightened up and looked at Cyl and me. "If y'all'll give me your keys, I'll go move your cars."

"Why?" I asked. "We're not blocking you, are we?"

"No, but they're right under those big oaks and the way this wind's blowing, you might be better off out in the open."

We immediately handed them over. By the time he came back, soaked to the skin, we were putting the food on the table. He quickly changed into some of Daddy's clothes and put his own in the dryer.

Daddy likes to pray about as much as he likes talking on the telephone, but with Maidie and the children sitting there with bowed heads, the rest of us followed their example and he offered up his usual, "For what we are about to receive, O Lord, make us truly thankful. Amen."

"Amen," we said and passed the bowls and platters. The biscuits were hot and flaky. The chicken was crisp on the outside, tender and juicy on the inside— ambrosia from the southern part of heaven.

Stan was a little more polite about it than Reese, but both ate as if it was their first meal in three days.

"Did you know that Edwards woman that got killed in Cotton Grove last night?" Reese asked Maidie as he spooned a third helping of potato salad onto his plate.

I was sitting next to him and I gave his thigh a sharp nudge.

"Let's don't talk about that right now," I said warningly.

Luckily, Lashanda had been distracted by Ladybelle, who knows better than to beg food from any of us, but couldn't be prevented from sitting near any newcomer in the hope that she might not know the rules. Stan had heard though, and his eyes widened. He turned to Cyl, who sat on the other side of him, and she nodded gravely.

Suddenly he didn't seem to be hungry any more and when he asked to be excused so he could go check on what Fran was doing, Cyl went with him.

Reese and Maidie picked up that something was going on and they kept Lashanda laughing and talking and plied with honey for her biscuit till Cyl came back to the table.

We were more than halfway through the dishes when the power went off, plunging us into darkness deeper than most of us had seen since the last power outage. What with security lights and even streetlights popping up all over the area, we don't get much true darkness anymore. Daddy had a flashlight to hand and once the candles and lanterns had been lit, Maidie insisted we go ahead and finish washing up while the water system still had enough pressure to do the job.

Power failure rules immediately went into effect: boys in the upstairs bathroom, girls in the downstairs and no flushing unless absolutely necessary, using water dipped from the full tubs.

Daddy and Cletus had moved into the den recliners and were regaling Stan with well-worn memories of Hurricane Hazel. Maidie's only about fifteen years older than me, so her memories of Hazel are pretty vague, but Cletus has another six or eight years on her and can match Daddy tree for fallen tree.

The candlelight soon took Daddy even further back, back before electricity came to this area.

"We didn't even have radio when I was a little fellow," he reminisced. "I was near-bout grown 'fore I heared it the first time. Seventy-five years ago, they was no weather satellites and the weather bureau did a lot of its predicting by what ships out at sea telegraphed to shore about the weather where they was. Way back here in the woods, we didn't know it was hurricanes stomping around out off the coast yonder. Old-timers used to call 'em August blows, 'cause most years, come late August, we'd get days and days of wind out of the northeast and sometimes we'd get a bunch of rain with it. A lot of times though, the sky'd be just as blue as you please, and that wind a-blowing."

As he spoke, the wind was blowing again, rattling the old wooden windows in their loose-fitting casements, and Lashanda tugged at my shirt. "Did you bring my baby doll, Miss Deborah?"

It was the first time I'd thought of it since I put the damp doll dress in my dryer. "Oh, honey, I'm so sorry. I went and left it at my house."

"Is that far away?" she asked plaintively.

"Not too far," I said brightly. "Why don't I just run over and get it for you."

"Here now," said Daddy. "I don't think that's a real smart idea. Wind catch hold of that little car of your'n and no telling where you'll fetch up."

"I'll carry her in my truck," said Reese, who seemed to have taken a shine to the child. "It's heavy enough. We won't be more'n a minute."

Before Daddy could order us not to go, Reese and I had grabbed flashlights and were out the back door, dashing across the yard to his truck. Umbrellas were

219

useless in this wind and neither of us bothered with one. The ground was soft and soggy and squished with each running step I took. Reese's white truck has such oversized tires that I almost needed a stepladder to swing up into the cab. There was a time when he wouldn't have let my wet clothes and muddy shoes into his truck. But that was before a deer tore the living bejeesus out of his beautiful leather seat covers and headliner last fall. Vinyl replacements were all he could afford and nowadays he's not quite as particular about water and dirt.

"We better not try going through the woods," Reese said, throwing the truck into four-wheel drive before we were even out of the yard.

Instead, he took the long way, through drag rows and lanes that bordered the fields. It was an exciting ride. Treetops were whipping in the wind, rain was coming down in buckets, and green leaves and pine needles were hurled so thickly against the windshield, the wipers almost couldn't handle them.

"Aren't you scared?" Reese asked, almost shouting to be heard above the rain pounding on the cab roof as we skidded through a cut in the woods that was almost blocked by a large pine limb.

I just laughed, feeling more alive than I had in ages. This was more exhilarating than a roller coaster.

As we turned out into the next field and followed the lane that runs alongside the pond, we saw car lights suddenly come on at the back of my house. We thought it might be one of the family, but instead of waiting for us or coming to meet us, it sped away down my driveway toward the road. By the time we got up to the house, the taillights were long gone, but the glare of Reese's lights showed that the door of my house was standing wide open. The window beside it had been smashed so that someone could reach inside and unlock the door.

Wind and rain were howling through the rooms. We slammed the door, then Reese headed through the kitchen to the garage for a tarp to nail over the window. When he brought it back, it was like hanging on to a sail even though my porch is roofed and screened. I had to pull the tarp taut and hold the flashlight steady, too, so he could see to nail.

As soon as that was taken care of, Reese lit the kerosene lamp on my kitchen counter and we shone our flashlights through the rest of the house to see what had been taken. Wind funnelling through the open door had scattered stuff, but no real damage had been done and I couldn't immediately see that the house had been seriously tossed. My few bits of real jewelry were untouched in the case on my dresser and all of Mother's sterling silver seemed to be occupying their proper compartments in the flannel-lined drawers.

The cards, pictures and bills from Clara Freeman's wallet had blown onto the floor, yet all were still there, including a five and two tens.

"We must've scared him off 'fore he could grab anything," said Reese.

I finished laying Clara's things back on fresh dry paper towels, then shone my light around the floor for items I might have missed.

"What you looking for?" asked my nephew.

"There were two envelopes," I said. "Here's the light bill, but the other one—"

I widened my search over every square inch of the area, to no avail. The damp envelope that had been sealed with Scotch tape was definitely gone.

At that instant, it was as if a flashbulb suddenly exploded in my head. *This* was why my car had been broken into? Looking for Clara Freeman's purse and the envelope? What could have been in it? And more importantly, who knew I had it?

Millard King had been there with Jason Bullock and me when I fished it out of the car. And at the hospital this morning, Dr. Jeremy Potts was standing beside Ralph Freeman when I said I had Lashanda's doll and Clara's purse.

"But not Brandon Frazier," whispered the preacher.

"And not Reid," said his headmate.

Until that moment of giddy relief, I hadn't realized how much I'd been subconsciously worrying about that dent in the right front fender of Reid's black BMW.

I was uneasy about leaving my house unprotected, but Reese wasn't about to let me stay.

"Granddaddy'll have my hide if I come back without you," he said.

I stuck the doll and its clothes into a plastic bag so it wouldn't get wet and we drove down my long rutted driveway just to make sure the intruder was well and truly gone. Normally, our sandy soil slurps up water like a sponge. Tonight, the wheel ruts were overflowing channels. Just as we paused before pulling onto the hardtop, the big wisteria-covered pine tree beside my mailbox crashed down across the driveway behind us, rocking the truck as its lower limb swiped the tail-gate. Two seconds earlier and we'd have been smashed beneath it.

"Holy shit!" Reese yelped and floored the accelerator.

"Watch out!" I shrieked and he almost put us in the ditch when he swerved to miss a limb lying in our lane. "Dammit, Reese, if you can't handle the speed, slow down!"

He did, but he was still shaking his head at two close calls.

"Well, one thing about it," he said sheepishly. "You don't have to worry about that guy coming back tonight. Nobody's gonna get through your lane without a chain saw or a bulldozer."

It was a short wild ride back to the homeplace. Along the way, I cautioned him not to talk about the break-in to Lashanda. "She's handling the storm and what's happened to her mother pretty good, but too much more might set her off."

"She knew the Edwards woman?" he asked.

"Her mother's best friend," I told him.

As we pulled up to the back porch, I was surprised to see Dwight's patrol car.

"I was about to send Dwight looking for you," Daddy said when Reese and I were back inside and I had handed Lashanda her doll.

"What're you doing out in this weather?" I asked him curiously.

Dwight shrugged. "This and that. And by the time I was ready to head back to Dobbs, I realized I might better stay the night out here at Mother's. Just thought I'd check on y'all since it's on my way."

I walked out to the shadowy kitchen with him and we paused at the doorway. In low tones, I told him about the intruder at my house, about the missing envelope and who knew I had Clara Freeman's purse, ending with my theory that that's why my trunk was popped.

"Dr. Jeremy Potts was standing right there when I told Ralph Freeman I'd forgotten to bring the purse in with me. I meant into Dobbs. If it *is* Potts, he might've thought I meant in from the car."

"Potts?" Dwight asked blankly. "What's he got to do with the price of eggs?"

I gave him a quick rundown on the Potts divorce and how Lynn Bullock found the argument that let Jason vacuum the good doctor's assets. "And Amy said he was downright gloating when he contributed to her memorial fund yesterday."

"Millard King did say he thought there was a doctor out on the running track with him," Dwight mused. "Maybe I'd better have a talk with Potts. And I'll definitely send someone out tomorrow to dust your kitchen and that purse."

He glanced over my shoulder to the cozy candlelit scene in the den.

Cyl and Stan were lounging at opposite ends of the opened couch with his battery-powered radio turned low to catch the latest storm updates. Reese sat on the floor nearby, absently strumming soft chords on my guitar. Maidie was crocheting almost by touch alone in one of the wooden rockers. Candles threw exaggerated shadows on the wall and Daddy and Cletus were amusing Lashanda by making shadow birds and animals with their hands. Some of their creations took all four hands and were quite complicated.

"Almost wish I was staying," Dwight said wistfully as he opened the door and stepped onto the porch.

The door was on the leeward side of the wind, and I walked out onto the porch with him. Between candles and kerosene lanterns, the house was starting to get too warm and stuffy and I was so glad for the fresh air that I continued to stand there with rainwater cascading off the porch roof while Dwight dashed out to his cruiser and drove away.

And I was still standing there three minutes later when the cruiser returned.

"This should teach me to be careful what I ask for," Dwight said wryly when he rejoined me on the porch. He dried his face on the shoulder of his wet sports shirt. "Two of Mr. Kezzie's pecan trees are laying across the lane and I can't get out. Use your phone?"

"If it's still working."

It was. First he called Miss Emily to say he wouldn't be coming after all. Too late. She'd left a message for him on her answering machine that Rob and Kate had insisted she spend the night with them and that he should come, too. Rob is Dwight's younger brother and lives just down the road from their mother in a big old farmhouse that Kate inherited from her first husband.

He dialled their number and had just explained about Daddy's pecan trees when the phone went dead in his ear.

Which meant he had to struggle back out to his

cruiser to radio the departmental dispatcher and let them know his location.

I had thought the rain was coming down as hard as it could possibly fall, but suddenly it was as if all the firehoses of heaven were pouring down on the back-yard. Even in such utter darkness, the cruiser's interior light was only a faint glow through the heavy sheets of water and Dwight was wetter than if he'd gone into the pond fully dressed.

"You people keep going in and out and Mr. Kezzie ain't gonna have no clothes left," Maidie grumbled as she fetched dry pants and shirt.

When I invited the Freeman kids to come to a hurri-cane party, I'd expected a mildly exciting storm. Fran would come ashore, I thought, and immediately col-lapse—lots of rain, a little wind, a brief power outage so we could have candles, maybe even a few dead twigs to clatter down across the old tin roof.

I did *not* expect the eye to come marching up I-40 straight through Colleton County, wreaking as much damage as Sherman's march through Georgia. Yet, as Stan's radio made clear, that was exactly what was hap-pening.

The storm hit Wilmington around nine, packing winds of a hundred and five miles per hour, and barely faltered as it moved across land on a north-by-northwest heading. By midnight, rain seemed to be coming down horizontally. It kept us busy stuffing newspapers and towels around door and window sills on the northeast side of the house.

"Good thing your mama never wanted wall-to-wall carpet," Daddy told me.

The house creaked like a ship at sea, then shuddered as a tree crashed onto the porch. We grabbed our flashlights, peered through the front windows and found the porch completely covered with the leaf-heavy top of an oak. At least two support posts had collapsed under the weight. Lashanda's eyes were wide with apprehension and she attached herself firmly to Cyl's side.

Dwight, Reese and Stan went up to the attic to check on the gable vents and Reese came back immediately for hammer, nails, and large plastic garbage bags.

"Rain's coming in through that northeast vent like somebody's standing outside with a hose aimed straight at it," he said. "We're going to try to plug it up."

"How's the roof?" asked Daddy.

"So far, it seems to be holding."

There was no guitar or fiddle for us that night, though at one point, Reese did manage to distract Lashanda with train sounds on his harmonica.

WPTF ("We Protect The Family") was tracking the storm the old-fashioned way as people along the route called in to the AM radio station with reports of trees down, possible tornadoes, wind and rain damage, and barometric pressure all the way down to 48.4 inches.

Around two, the wind finally slacked off enough to be noticeable. Lashanda had fallen asleep with one arm around Ladybelle and the other hugging her doll. Reese, too, was snoring on a pallet in the corner.

Daddy stood up stiffly and said, "Well, if that's the worst it's gonna do, I reckon I'll go lay down and get a little rest."

Maidie and Cletus followed him upstairs to real beds.

Stan lay on his pallet, fighting to stay awake enough to jot notes from the radio reports.

Cyl, Dwight and I went out to the kitchen where I boiled water for coffee. (With the power going off so often, a lot of us have our own LP tanks and cook with gas.) Dwight was hungry again, so I set out leftover fried chicken and the fixings for tomato sandwiches.

While he ate and Cyl and I drank coffee, we talked about the two killings—Lynn Bullock and Rosa Edwards—and whether Clara Freeman's wreck had anything to do with either of them.

"Which happened first?" I asked, trying to make sense of it. "The wreck or the Edwards killing?"

"If she went into Possum Creek immediately after leaving Miz Thomas, then that was first," said Dwight, "because Rosa Edwards worked her regular shift yesterday."

I tried doing a timetable. "So say Clara Freeman crashed her car around noon. It probably wouldn't take an hour to zoom out here from Dobbs at the precise moment and get back again, but how would anybody know where she was unless they'd spent the morning trailing her? Reid and Millard King were both roaming in and out of my courtroom all morning. Even Brandon Frazier came up during the lunch break to get me to sign a pleading, so unless Dr. Potts—"

"Wait, wait, wait!" Cyl protested. "Brandon Frazier? Millard King? Reid Stephenson? Your cousin? What do they have to do with the wreck or last night's murder?"

We'd forgotten that she wasn't up to speed on this.

"Rosa Edwards worked at the Orchid Motel. We think she saw Lynn Bullock's killer, and each of those three men slept with Lynn Bullock in the last few months," I said bluntly.

"Really?" Despite her own situation, Cyl frowned in distaste. All the men were familiar courthouse regulars, but she hadn't known Jason Bullock's wife. "Was she such a fox?" Cyl asked curiously. "Or such a slut?"

Dwight and I both shrugged. "Some of both probably," I said.

Interrupting each other, he and I almost did a probable cause on each man and how none of them had a watertight alibi for the time of death—between five and eight on Saturday evening. As rain pounded against the window glass, we discussed Millard King's desire for future elective office, Reid's late arrival and early departure from the field, Brandon Frazier's frank admissions, and the tie tack that probably belonged to Millard King. (I busied myself tidying the table while Dwight told her about the silver pen.)

"What about her husband—Jason Bullock? Did you eliminate him?"

I explained how I was there when Lynn Bullock called, pretending to be a hundred miles away and how he'd been at the field during the relevant times.

"She was registered under her maiden name, and some man called the motel switchboard before she checked in and again just a few minutes after she talked to Jason. Asked for her by the name she was using, too."

"Might as well tell her about Jeremy Potts, too," said Dwight. "Deborah thinks—"

At that moment, we were startled when the back door opened with a loud squeak and something dark and shiny walked in from the storm. In the flickering candlelight, it gave the three of us a start till we realized it was Cletus, wearing a large black plastic garbage bag for a rain poncho.

"I thought you went up to bed," I said.

"Naw, I got to worrying about how the house was faring down there. Went out the side door. They's a tree down across the path now, so I had to come back in this way." He pulled off the bag and left it to drip in the sink before heading back upstairs. "You young folks oughta get a little rest. Be morning soon."

Physically, we were all tired but were too keyed up to call it a night just yet. And Cyl wanted to know about Jeremy Potts. Once again, I found myself describing that acrimonious divorce and Lynn Bullock's part in it.

I finished up by reminding her that she was there at the hospital when I told Ralph that I had his wife's handbag. "And less than forty-five minutes later, somebody popped the lock on my car trunk."

"Looking for her purse? But why?" Cyl asked. "And why would anybody hurt Ralph's wife if this Rosa Edwards was the one who could put him at the motel?"

"Maybe he was afraid Rosa had talked to her good friend Clara," I said. "I don't know."

"We do know that she was driving Mrs. Freeman's car last Saturday," Dwight reminded me.

"So maybe he thought she was the one who'd seen him."

"*If* anyone saw him," Cyl said, sounding like a skeptical prosecutor. "Coincidences do happen and—"

Yawning widely, Stan came out to the kitchen. "They say the eye just collapsed over Garner a few minutes ago. I guess it's pretty much over."

His own eyes were looking at the chicken with such interest that I got him a paper plate, napkins, and a big glass of milk to go with it. He wasn't interested in a tomato sandwich, "but if there's any of that potato salad left?"

There was.

When his plate was full, Stan looked around the table. "Miss Cyl told me about Miss Rosa getting killed. Is that what y'all were talking about?"

We admitted we were.

"When did you last see her?" I asked.

"Deborah!" Cyl protested. "He's a minor."

"And if Ralph were here, do you think he'd object to Stan telling us that?"

"It's okay, Miss Cyl," said Stan, using his paper napkin to wipe milk from his upper lip. "She came over to the house yesterday morning just as Mama was fixing to drive us to school. Shandy and I were already in the car, but Mama was still in the house and Miss Rosa just went on in. Said she had to speak to Mama about something."

"Did she say what about?" asked Dwight.

"No, sir. And Mama didn't say, either. They both came out together and Miss Rosa drove off and then Mama took us to school. That's the last time we saw her. I tried to call her when Mama went missing, but she never answered her phone. I guess she was working then?"

"Do you know where she works?" I interjected curiously.

He shook his head. "I think she's a housekeeper somewhere in Dobbs. One of the motels?"

Dwight gave me one of his do-you-mind? looks. "And all she said was that she had to speak to your mother? Those were her exact words? Nothing about why?"

Stan nibbled thoughtfully on the drumstick he held, then shook his head. "I'm sorry, no."

"Stan," I said slowly. "There was an envelope in your mother's purse and—"

"Hey, right!" His face brightened. "I forgot. When Miss Rosa went in the house, she was carrying a white envelope. And when she came back out, she wasn't. She must've given it to Mama. Did you open it? What was in it?"

"I didn't open it. Someone burgled my house tonight and took it."

"What?"

Cyl and Stan were both looking at me in disbelief.

"That's why Reese and I were so long getting back with Lashanda's doll," I said and told them about the broken window and fleeing taillights.

Cyl shook her head. "Girl, you do stay in the middle of things, don't you?"

"That's why Miss Rosa got killed, wasn't it?" asked Stan, making the same leap I'd made but not for the same reasons. If Lynn Bullock's murder over in Dobbs had even registered on him, it was clear he didn't connect it to Rosa Edwards. "She had something somebody wanted and she gave it to Mama to hold for her? And then when Mama disappeared, they must've thought Miss Rosa was lying about not being able to get it back?"

He yawned again. "I wonder if she told Mama what it was?" Suddenly he looked very young. "I sure hope she wakes up tomorrow."

"Today," said Cyl. "And you'd better get some sleep."

"You okay on that pallet?" I asked. "Or would you rather try one of the recliners?"

"The floor's fine," he said with yet another wide yawn that made me yawn, too.

Cyl and Dwight were smothering yawns of their own as Stan said goodnight and went to lie down in the den.

I opened the back door to let in some fresh air. It was only marginally cooler than the air inside and heavy with moisture. Rain still pounded the tin roof and fell as if it meant to go on falling forever.

Dwight's face was grim as he joined me by the doorway.

"It was her insurance policy, wasn't it?" I said.

"Probably."

"She told him she'd written it down and given it to someone to hold," Cyl said softly from behind us. "That's why he cut her so badly. And kept cutting till she told him who."

"Then killed her because he thought he'd already killed the who and sunk her purse," I said. "I wonder if Millard King really was visiting his brother in Fuquay last night or was he hanging around Possum Creek waiting to see if he could get to Clara Freeman's car before anyone else did?"

"If he was, it must've scared the hell out of him when you grabbed her purse," said Dwight with a wry smile.

"Unless it was Dr. Jeremy Potts," said Cyl. "Surgeons don't mind blood, do they?"

After Dwight went off to bed in my old corner room upstairs, Cyl and I changed into gym shorts and baggy T-shirts for sleeping. I turned the lantern wick down real low, then went around blowing out all the candles.

Stan had crawled under the sheet next to his little sister's feet and both children were breathing deeply.

I crawled onto my side of the couch. It felt wonderful to lie down.

I watched as Cyl untangled the top of the sheet from Lashanda's arm and moved Ladybelle away from her face, then came and stretched out beside me.

"They're really nice kids, aren't they?" she sighed.

"You're going to make a terrific mother someday," I told her.

"But not their mother." A great sadness was in her voice.

"They have a mother, Cyl."

"You think I don't know that?"

"But you can't help wishing—?"

"That they were mine?" She turned to me with a low moan. "Oh, God, Deborah, I'm such a horrible person!"

"No, you're not," I said, trying to comfort her. "You didn't mean to fall in love with Ralph. You didn't set out to snare him or anything. It just happened."

"That's not what I mean."

"What then?"

She was silent for a long moment and when she finally did speak, her voice was so hushed I had to strain to hear her.

"When I heard that she was hurt—in a coma— I thought, What if she never wakes up? What if she just goes ahead and dies?" She looked at me and her eyes were dark pools of despair in the dim light. "What kind of a monster could wish for something like that?"

"You're no monster," I said. "You're only human."

"I thought that . . . in the end, he'd choose love," she whispered. "Our love. But now she's hurt so bad. It could take her months, years, to recover. He'll never leave her like that. He couldn't do it to his children."

Tears spilled down her cheeks.

"And neither could I."

"What will you do?"

She shook her head helplessly. "All I know is that I can't stay here. I can give him up, but not if I stay here."

She began to cry and her muffled sobs tore at my heart.

I felt movement at the end of the couch, then Lashanda was there between us on the sofa bed. She patted Cyl's cheek tenderly.

"Don't cry, Miss Cyl. It'll soon be morning."

CHAPTER 17

Is it at all wonderful that, after the strain
was over and all danger gone, reason
should finally be unseated and men and
women break into the unmeaning gayety
of the maniac?

We awoke on Friday morning to sunshine, dead still
mugginess and the sound of chain saws and tractors.
Trees were down all around the house. We'd had so
much rain these last few weeks and the ground was so
saturated that roots had pulled right out of the earth
in Fran's high sustained winds. The children were already outdoors and Cyl and I got a cup of coffee and
went out to survey the damage more closely. Lashanda
immediately ran to greet us.

Mother's magnolias still stood tall and proud, although one had been skinned the full length of its
trunk when a neighboring pine fell over.

"We'll prune it up. See if we can save it," said my brother Seth, giving me a sweaty morning hug.

His mother, Daddy's first wife, hadn't found the time to worry about landscaping, so it was my mother who planted azaleas and dogwoods and magnolias with the help of her stepsons who came to love her as their own. Seth could remember the first year the magnolias bloomed and how their fragrance drifted through the bedroom windows at night, bewitching their dreams.

He, Robert and Haywood were there to help Daddy clear the drive so we could get in and out. The tree across the porch looked awful, but the actual damage was minimal and would have to wait in line since there was worse to be taken care of on the farm.

Reese's place was the hardest hit. Two sixty-foot pines had crashed down on the trailer he was renting from Seth and everything he owned was either smashed or waterlogged. Seth had insurance on the trailer itself, but Reese had nothing on the contents. "First my truck, now my trailer," he said gloomily.

He'd already been over to the wreckage this morning and the back of his pickup was loaded with wet clothes, tapes and CDs, and other odds and ends that were salvageable. Daddy'd told him to come stay at the homeplace till he could figure out what he wanted to do.

Andrew and April were hard hit, too. A huge oak had taken out the whole northwest side of their house, shearing off the kitchen and dining room wall.

"You know April, though," said Seth with a grin. "She's already talking about how she's been wanting to get more light into that part of the house and now the insurance money will help her do it."

(April moves walls in that house like other women move furniture.)

In addition to Reese's trailer, Seth was mourning four mature pecans. Haywood said he had nineteen trees down in his yard, but none of them hit the house. Robert hadn't counted his downed trees, "but the yard's full of 'em," and they said that the farm's biggest potato house had lost three sheets of tin off the roof.

("I've heard of being three sheets in the wind," Haywood chuckled, "but I didn't know they was talking about tin sheets.")

Other than a little water damage, most of the other houses on the farm, including my own, were pretty much unscathed.

The roads were blocked all around, they said, but neighbors were out, working on getting at least one lane cleared.

Power was still off and phones were out over most of the county. Even cell phones were spotty, depending on which company you were with. Dwight had already used his car radio to send word to Ralph Freeman at the hospital that Stan and Lashanda were fine, and word had come back that Ralph would try to get home to Cotton Grove by mid-morning to meet them there.

I managed to get through to Aunt Zell on my cell phone, even though it was staticky and other voices kept fading in and out. She said most of Dobbs was without power but the phones were still working. She'd been worried since she hadn't heard from any of us. I assured her that we were all physically fine.

"What about y'all?" I asked. "Everything okay there?"

"Not exactly," she admitted. "Your Uncle Ash put our new Lincoln in the garage last night and left the old one sitting in the drive. You remember that big elm out by the edge of the yard? It totalled the garage and our new car both. Not a scratch on the old one. Ash is so provoked."

I could imagine.

"And Portland called this morning. Remember how she and Avery fetched their boat home to get it out of harm's way?"

I had to laugh. "Don't tell me."

"Yep. A pine tree cut it right half in two."

Lashanda followed us around the yard, chattering sixty to the dozen, but Stan stayed busy helping the menfolks till Maidie called us in for sausage and griddle cakes.

There was no school, of course, and no court either, for that matter. Seth had brought over a battery-powered radio for Daddy and we listened open-mouthed to the reports coming in from around the area. Fran never made it beyond a category 3 storm, but it had moved across the state so slowly that it did much more damage than a stronger, faster-moving hurricane would have. Even more than legendary Hazel, they were saying. Most of the problems seemed to have been caused by trees falling on cars, houses and power lines. And there was quite a bit of flooding in low-lying areas.

"You'll probably have the most dramatic science project in your class," Cyl told Stan.

"Sounds like an A to me, too," I said.

"Maybe," he said, not meeting our eyes.

Andrew and A.K arrived with news that at least one lane of Highway 48 was clear in either direction and that they'd also heard it was possible to drive to Cotton Grove on Old 48.

"Reckon I'll be going then," said Dwight. "If Stan and Lashanda are ready to go, I can drop them off."

Stan immediately put down his fork and stood up, but I said, "That's okay. Cyl and I'll take them. Ralph's probably not home yet and Stan needs to get all his notes and books together, so we won't hold you up."

He and my brothers, Daddy and Cletus went back outside. Maidie was putting together the scraps of breakfast ham to take down to the caged hunting beagles.

"Why don't you let Lashanda help you?" I asked with a meaningful cut of my eyes that Maidie read like a book.

As soon as Cyl and I were alone with Stan, I said, "What's wrong?"

"Nothing," he answered sullenly. At eleven, almost twelve, he might have a man's height, but he was still a boy, a boy who wanted to play it cool, yet was still too inexperienced not to show his raw emotions. He pushed away from the table and walked into the den area to gather up his things.

Cyl shot me an apprehensive glance as we followed him in and began folding up the bedclothes.

"Did you hear us talking last night?" I asked him bluntly.

"What if I did?" he said, his back to us.

"Did you understand what you heard?"

Angry and confused, he turned on Cyl. "I liked you! I thought you were our friend."

"I liked you too, Stan," she said sadly. "I still do."

"But you—? With my dad? While Mama's lying there hurt?"

"What happened was before she was hurt," Cyl said.

"But you want her dead!"

Cyl shook her head. "No, I don't."

"If you heard us talking," I said, "then you heard that it's over. Almost before it began. Stan—?"

He didn't want to listen and when Cyl put her hand out to him, he backed away from her.

"I know you're upset about your mom," she said. "Mad at me and mad at your dad, and I can't blame you for that. I'm not even going to try and ask you to understand, but—"

"Good!" he said hotly. "Because I don't. And don't try saying it's because I'm too young either!"

"I wasn't." She finished folding a quilt, laid it on the growing stack I'd begun, and took a deep breath. "What happened between your father and me happened. It can't ever be undone, but it *is* over. Finished. It doesn't have to affect you and your sister unless you let it fester. What I'm asking is that you keep it between your father and me. Talk to him if you need to talk about it, but don't bring anybody else into it. Especially your mom."

"Yeah, I just bet you don't want her to know!" he said angrily. "But she has a right to. She *needs* to!"

"No, she doesn't."

"But—"

"You said you don't want to be treated like a child, Stan."

"I don't."

"Then you're going to have to think before you speak. And you're going to have to realize that the hardest thing about being grown up is keeping hurtful things to yourself. You think you can get rid of a hurt like this by giving it to your mother?" She shook her head sadly. "It doesn't work like that, Stan. You won't divide the hurt you're feeling, you'll only double it. Do you really want to do that to her?"

Anguish mingled with resentment in the boy's eyes.

"No, ma'am," he said at last.

Cyl and I drove Stan and Lashanda back to Cotton Grove in mid-morning. Angry and confused as he was, he was still young enough to be as distracted as his little sister by all the devastation. And it truly was amazing. Andrew and A.K. had been told that it was possible to drive Old 48 into town, and it was. But only because we kept detouring and backtracking. We had heard reports of tornadoes in the night and now we could see where small ones might have touched down: swaths of woodlands where treetops had been twisted off still-standing trunks.

Trunks and limbs were everywhere. Power poles were down. Every fifth house seemed to have a big leafy tree on it somewhere, mostly on the roof, but also through windows and across porches and cars. Yet, considering the number of trees that had fallen, it was amazing how many did *not* hit houses. I had to drive slowly because the roads were often single lanes and clogged with other drivers who were out to survey the damage before tackling their own.

As we entered town, an almost festive air hung over the streets. Everyone seemed to be out sightseeing along the sidewalks and the mood was one of good-natured excitement. Children clambered on fallen tree trunks, chattering and pointing. Neighbors called out to other neighbors who drove past with rolled-down windows despite the hot and muggy day. Part of it was amazement at so much destruction, another part had to be relief that the destruction wasn't worse. As we crept along at a snail's pace, I did my own share of exchanging news.

"Hey, there, Deb'rah," folks would call. "Mr. Kezzie okay?"

"He's fine," I'd call back. "Y'all come through it all right? Anybody have power yet?"

"Not on this side of town. Heared it's back on from North Main to the town limits, though."

More detours through parts of Cotton Grove I hadn't visited in ages, more waits for our turn to pass through the single open lanes.

"Isn't that Jason Bullock?" asked Cyl as we were routed down an unfamiliar street.

I followed her pointing finger and there he was, coming along the driveway of a nondescript house and carrying a chain saw and gas can.

He saw us at the same time and walked over to my open window. His blue T-shirt was drenched with perspiration, flecks of sawdust sprinkled his brown hair and I smelled the strong odor of gasoline from his chain saw.

"Ms. DeGraffenried, Judge. This is really something, isn't it?"

"That your house?" I asked. "Doesn't look like you had much damage."

He laughed. "Look a little closer. See that brush pile? I just finished cutting it off my car. You can't see it from here, but the top's got a dent the size of a fish pond and the side's smashed in. Still, I was luckier than Mrs. Wesley down there." He gestured to a house half a block further on, where an enormous oak had pulled out of the ground and crushed the front of a shabby old two-story frame house that had seen better days. "She's eighty-three and her only relative's the seventy-year-old niece who lives with her. Some of the neighbors and I are fixing to clear their yard for them."

By this time, Lashanda had slipped out of her seat belt and was kneeling on the backseat with her forearms on the back of my seat and her small face next to mine.

"Hey, there," she said.

Jason smiled down at her, then said to Cyl, "These aren't your children, are they?"

She shook her head. "No."

"Actually, though, you need to meet them," I said. "Lashanda, Stan, this is Mr. Bullock. He's one of the men from the rescue squad that pulled your mother out of the creek night before last."

Before he or Stan could respond, Lashanda said, "Do you have a little girl, too?"

"Nope, I'm afraid not," said Jason.

As the cars ahead of me began to move, we said goodbye and he stood back, so we could drive on.

From the backseat, I heard Stan say, "You know him?"

"Not really. Can you do my seat belt? I can't click it."

"Then how come you thought he had a daughter?"

" 'Cause when Mama comes to pick me up at school, he's there, too."

Despite the heat, a chill went down my spine at the child's words. Making my voice as casual as I could, I said, "You've seen him at your school, honey?"

"Yes'm, and guess what? When we stop for groceries and stuff, he goes to the same places."

Cyl glanced at me curiously and then her eyes widened as she picked up on what I was thinking.

Goes to the same places? Childless, white Jason Bullock "goes to the same places" as Clara Freeman, a black mother?

My mind raced across the events of the last week, fitting one fact with another as everything spun like the wheels of a slot machine planning to come up cherries straight across. Unfortunately, it was another four minutes to the Freeman house and I couldn't say a word to Cyl.

Ralph and his father-in-law were getting out of the car when we drove up. A chinaball tree had blown down near the carport, just missing one of the support posts, but that seemed to be the only damage here.

By the set of his chin, I saw that Stan meant to step between Cyl and his father so I quickly loaded him down with his and Lashanda's overnight backpacks and asked where he wanted his radio as I carried it up to the side door. Too well-mannered to dig in his heels, he reluctantly followed Lashanda and me up the drive. I greeted a weary Reverend Gaithers with burbling cheerfulness, asked about Clara, and said how much we'd enjoyed having the two kids. All this so that Cyl could have one very quick, if very public, moment with Ralph.

"She's doing better," said the old man. "I really do believe the good Lord's going to spare her. She opened her eyes this morning for a few minutes. I don't know if she knew me, but when I squeezed her hand, she squeezed mine back."

As we stood talking, the kids went on into the house and began opening all the windows, not that there was any breeze to mitigate the smothering, humidity-drenched heat. A chain saw three doors down made it difficult to understand each other and when it paused, I heard the siren of a rescue vehicle rushing somewhere several streets over. Ralph came up the drive and it was hard to meet his eyes as I told him I was glad to hear that his wife seemed to be coming out of her coma.

"Did you tell him Stan knows?" I asked Cyl as we drove away.

She nodded. "I'd give anything to take that knowledge away from him."

"Ralph? Or Stan?"

"Stan."

I started to speak, but she said, "I don't want to talk about it anymore, okay?"

"Okay." I paused at the stop sign, trying to remember precisely how we'd come. "Jason Bullock's car is black," I said.

"I noticed."

"Want to bet he's already lined up a body shop to get the dents banged out and repainted?"

"No bets." She sighed and I wondered if that sigh was for Ralph or Jason.

Either way, I reached over and squeezed her hand.

"I guess I don't have all the facts straight," Cyl said gamely, trying to match my interest in Lynn Bullock's murder. "How could Jason be at the motel killing his wife at the very same time he's at the ball field playing ball?"

I'd already figured it out.

"Remember last night?" I told her. "How we thought Cletus was upstairs asleep? If anybody'd asked me to alibi him, I'd have taken my oath he was there all the time, wouldn't you?"

"I guess."

"Well, it's the same with Jason Bullock. I heard him get a call from his wife around five and he was there for pregame pictures around six-thirty. He wandered down for a Coke, and I saw him talking to people on his way to the rest area, but he could have slipped away for a half-hour and who would notice? I wonder if he got a little too cute, though?"

"How do you mean?"

"The switchboard says a man called the motel twice—right before she checked in and again after she called Jason. If he got cocky and made those calls from his cell phone, there'll be a record of it on his bill. Reid, Millard King, and Brandon Frazier all say she wouldn't give them the time of day anymore. Maybe she really had quit messing around with other men."

Cyl nodded thoughtfully. "So she went to that motel expecting Jason to join her for a romantic tryst after his ball game, perhaps trying to put the spark back into their marriage?"

Our line of work made us familiar with the sexual games some couples play.

"And Jason used it to set up her death. Reid says he's ambitious, and he's certainly bright enough to see how a woman like Lynn could hold him back. The way she dressed, the way she'd slept with half the bar in Colleton County? He could divorce her, but then he'd be in the same spot as Dr. Jeremy Potts. Everybody knows Lynn put him through law school. He wouldn't want to pay alimony the rest of his life based on his enhanced income potential, now would he?"

"But Rosa Edwards saw him and he came after her," said Cyl.

"Only first, he came after an African-American woman driving a white Honda Civic," I said.

Cyl's lovely mobile face froze as the implications of my words sank in.

"Of course," she said bitterly. "He didn't run Clara Freeman into the creek, it was the car and whatever black woman happened to be driving that car. We probably all look alike to him."

The street ahead led straight out of town and seemed to be clear as far as I could see. Nevertheless, I turned left, retracing our trek through town.

"Why are we going this way?" asked Cyl.

"Because I want another look at Jason Bullock's car. It seems to me that that was an awfully small tree to have done that much damage. Maybe he helped it along with a sledgehammer or something."

"And you want to play detective? No. Call the Sheriff's Department. Let Dwight Bryant handle it. I mean it, Deborah. I want to go home."

"It won't take but a minute," I soothed.

But as we turned into Jason's street, we immediately ran into a solid wall of cars and people, all focused on the rescue truck halfway down the block.

"Oh, Lord," said Cyl. "That's where they were going to cut up a tree. Did that old woman have a heart attack or somebody get hurt?"

With the crowd watching whatever fresh disaster was unfolding, it seemed like a good time to slip over and take a closer look at Jason's car. Accordingly, I copied several other vehicles and parked diagonally with two wheels on the pavement and the other two on someone's front lawn.

"Be right back," I told Cyl, who grabbed at a nearby woman's arm, to ask what was going on. I saw men running with shovels from all over and I hesitated, finally registering the naked horror that hung palpably in the air.

A man I recognized by face though not by name was backing out of the crowd. He was built like a bear with thick neck and brawny arms and he was covered with sawdust and a cold sweat. His eyes were glazed, his face was greenish white. I couldn't tell if he was in shock or about to throw up.

"What happened?" I asked.

"Oh, God! I didn't know he was down there. I didn't know!"

"Know what?" I asked again.

"The stump just stood back up."

I couldn't make sense of his words, but someone who knew him hurried out of the crowd and put his arm around the man and told me to leave him alone. "Come away, Fred. It's not your fault. The damn fool shouldn't have been down there."

If Fred couldn't talk, there were others almost hysterical at witnessing such a ghastly accident. A hundred-year-old oak had pulled halfway out of the ground, they said, leaving behind a huge root hole, several feet across and three or four feet deep. A neighbor had gone into the hole and was bending down to cut through the roots that were still in the ground just as another neighbor—the man they called Fred—finished cutting through the trunk's three-foot diameter.

Released from the weight of those heavy, leaf-laden branches, the thick stump and enormous root ball suddenly flipped back into the hole, completely burying the man who was there. A dozen men were digging with shovels and picks, others were trying to hitch ropes and chains from the stump to a team of pickup trucks. They had sent for a bulldozer that was even now lumbering down the street, but everyone knew it was too late the instant the stump righted itself.

"That poor bastard!" said one of the men. "First his wife and now him."

"Such a good man," said an elderly white woman with tears running down her face. "He was always looking to help others."

Before I could ask the final question, Cyl pulled me away.

"It's Jason Bullock," she said.

CHAPTER | 18

Most of these storms describe a parabola, with the westward arch touching the Atlantic Coast, after which the track is northeastward, finally disappearing with the storm itself in the north Atlantic.

With Jason Bullock dead, there was no way to know whether Cyl and I were right about his reasons for killing his wife—anger over Lynn's affairs, political aspirations, or a simple wish to be free of her without paying the price of divorce. The important thing was that once Dwight's people concentrated on him, there was plenty of proof that he had indeed done it.

I was right about his cell phone bills. He'd called the Orchid Motel from the ball field twice, trying to make it look as if another man knew she was there. We still don't know if he jogged over to the motel or drove. No witness has come forward to say they saw him do either, but there's at least a half-hour gap when none of us can say positively that he was at the field.

They haven't found the envelope Rosa Edwards gave Clara Freeman, but the bloody clothes he'd worn when he butchered her were in a garbage bag at the bottom of his trash barrel, so we're pretty sure he's the one who stole the envelope from my house. And as soon as Clara Freeman was well enough for Dwight to interview her, she described Jason's car and identified his picture as the white man who ran her off the road.

When Reid eventually heard that Millard King's tie tack had also been found in Lynn's motel room, he theorized that she must have had a cache of souvenirs and that Jason had planted them to implicate the men who had slept with his wife. He was real proud of his theory and ready to run tell it to Dwight until I reminded him why this would not be a good idea.

"But I could get my pen back," he argued.

"Forget it," I snarled.

Dwight beat up on himself when all the other facts were in. "Last time I believe a lawyer about anything," he said bitterly. "That night I went to tell him about his wife? If you could've seen it—table set for two, salad wilting in the bowl, steaks drying up on the drainboard—and just the right mixture of shock and anger. He played me like a goddamned violin."

"Or a jury," I said cynically.

Five hot and sweaty days later, power was still out over the rural parts of Colleton County, although phone service had been restored in less than forty-eight hours. Eighteen states had sent crews to help restore North Carolina's electricity but over five thousand

poles were down and at least three thousand miles of
wires and cables needed to be replaced.

Every day reminded us all over again just how much
we relied on electricity in ways we didn't even realize.
My family could be smug about cooking with propane
gas but in this heat, we were having trouble keeping
food fresh in our picnic coolers without a ready supply
of ice. Robert, Andrew and Haywood had portable
gas-run generators and were sharing them with Daddy
and Seth every eight hours so that nobody lost a
freezer chest full of meat and vegetables, but all the
gasoline pumps at the local crossroads stations worked
by electricity and for the first couple of days, lines were
long at the few in-town stations that hadn't lost
power.

We had to recharge our portable phones at work,
tell time by wristwatches, prise open windows that had
been painted shut after the advent of year-round "cli-
mate control," and swelter through long smothery
nights without even a ceiling fan to stir a breeze. We
had to think before flushing toilets and forget about
showers. Candlelight lost its romantic novelty after
two days and there was a lot of grumbling about
spending the evenings without any electronic enter-
tainments.

I cleaned out my refrigerator before it started
smelling and put trays of baking soda on the shelves so
that stale odors wouldn't build up. Some of my per-
ishables went to Aunt Zell's refrigerator over in
Dobbs. I started a compost pile with the rest.

Dobbs had gone without power a mere thirty-six
hours, but our courts were still on half-session.

On Thursday morning, I heard a probable cause

against a Norwood Love from down near Makely, who was represented by my cousin John Claude Lee. During the storm, the back of young Mr. Love's hog pen collapsed, revealing an underground chamber beneath the barn it abutted—a chamber full of large plastic barrels and a stainless steel cooker, all set to start making bootleg whiskey.

According to the agent who testified that morning, it did not appear that the still had ever been in operation, but mere possession of such equipment is against the law. I agreed that there was indeed probable cause and set a trial date. Since Mr. Love had no record, though, I released him without bail.

Afterwards, I visited with Aunt Zell to pick up a couple of loads of laundry that she'd done for Daddy and Maidie and me.

"If Kidd wants to come up this weekend, he can stay here," she offered, knowing how long it'd been.

I thanked her, but said I doubted he could get away.

Truth is, I wasn't sure if he wanted to get away.

We'd spoken a couple of times. I called him that first day to say I was all right, in case he was worried, and to hear how he was. What he was, was . . . shall we say, occupied?

The storm surge at New Bern was more than nine feet and it had flooded his daughter Amber and his ex-wife out of their house. Last time I phoned, they were both staying with Kidd, whose cabin was on higher ground. So maybe that was the reason he didn't sound anxious to come to me, and it was certainly the reason I couldn't go to him.

When I stopped past the homeplace to give Maidie

the folded laundry, I was surprised to see Daddy standing by an unfamiliar pickup.

It was an awkward moment as Norwood Love and I
recognized each other from morning court. He murmured a soft, "Sorry, ma'am," then cranked his truck
and drove off.

"How do you know him?" I asked Daddy.

"I know a lot of people, shug," he said.

"Did he tell you he's waiting trial for owning moonshining equipment?"

"Yeah, he told me." He gave a rueful shake of his
head. "Reckon that's why he come to me. Thought
maybe I'd understand quicker than most folks how
come he needs extra work. I said I'd hire him to clear
out some of them trees blocking the lanes. Your brothers got so much on their plates, we can use another
pair of hands."

Daddy doesn't often touch on his own past history
of moonshining and he's certainly never discussed it
with me even though I've heard a lot of the stories
from my brothers and a few others from SBI and ATF
agents. As I've gotten older and heard more, I have to
say that not all of the stories have been warm and
funny. Some have a violent edge that makes me uneasy
to think about.

There wasn't a breath of wind blowing when I got
back to my house and the air was so steamy that I
planned to jump into the pond as soon as I arrived.

Cyl was waiting for me on the porch. It was the first
time I'd seen her looking halfway like herself since the
storm, but then she lived in Garner where there was

hot and cold running water, air-conditioning and hair dryers.

"Want to go skinny-dipping?" I said as soon as I got out of the car.

"Not really."

There was something different about her.

"What's up?" I asked.

"I just came from my grandmother's and I wanted you to be the second to know."

"Know what?" I asked with apprehension.

"That I gave Doug Woodall my notice at noon today. I flew up to Washington yesterday to interview with McLean, Applebee and Shaw and they made me a very generous offer."

The name was vaguely familiar.

"They're one of the most effective black lobbyist firms in Washington," she said. "I'll be going back up this weekend to look for an apartment."

"Oh, Cyl," I said, "are you sure?"

"I'm sure," she said firmly. "I just wanted to thank you for being there when I really needed a friend."

My eyes filled with tears. It's in the genes. Half my family can't watch a Hallmark commercial without crying.

She was crisp and cool, I was hot and sweaty, but I hugged her anyhow. "I'm really going to miss you, girl."

"No, you won't. I'll be back to visit Grandma and you can come visit me. I'm hoping to find a place in Georgetown. Think of us in all those great shops and restaurants."

"Yeah," I said glumly.

"It's the only way I can deal with it," she said quietly and this time, she hugged me.

After Cyl left, I changed clothes, then got out the pane of glass and glazing putty I'd bought a couple of days ago and began repairing my broken window. Different brothers had offered to do it, but they're still working on bigger repairs. At least I don't have tall trees around my house to fall on anything. And maybe I ought to reconsider where I want to plant them. Dwight's right: it'll take twenty years to grow them tall enough to do any damage, but I'll probably still be here—alone—twenty years from now. Certainly doesn't look as if I'll be setting up housekeeping in New Bern any time soon.

I'm probably not cut out to be anybody's stepmom.

Unlike Cyl, who would have been terrific under different circumstances.

I hadn't seen Ralph Freeman since the day after the storm, but I heard that Clara was making a pretty good recovery, all things considered, and would probably be home before the weekend although Amy says she's going to need a lot of physical therapy in the next few months.

Reese came by for a swim just as I was ready to jump in myself. He said that a power crew from Virginia was working its way out from Cotton Grove.

"The way they're moving, we might get our lights back by midnight."

"And not a minute too soon," I said fervently as I floated on my back and let the warm water relax me.

"I'll tell you one good thing about Fran, though," he said, drifting along beside me.

"Yeah?"

"We're not gonna have to listen to any more Hazel stories any time soon, are we?"

I laughed. "And fifty years from now, if I catch you telling Fran stories to your grandbabies, I'll punch you hard."

Darkness fell much as it did a hundred years ago, quietly and utterly. The night sky was radiant with stars undimmed by electric yard lights or the streetlights going in across the creek where a new housing development's being built. Fireflies glowed with flicks of soft golden yellow while crickets sang to the stars.

It was the dark of the moon, yet the countryside seemed luminous to me. I blew out my candles and walked out to the pond, then skirted the edge and followed the rutted lane that was a double line of white sand against the darker grass.

Near the end of the pond, I smelled smoke and followed my nose till I saw fire reflected off bushes beyond the cut in the undergrowth. As I passed through the cut into the open field, I saw Daddy burning a brush pile and I couldn't help but smile. Other men burn brush in the daytime but Daddy's always done his burning at night. I watched him stir the flaming branches with his pitchfork. Sparks jetted thirty feet upwards like a fiery fountain against the velvet darkness.

Blue and Ladybelle came out to greet me, and as I walked into the circle of light, Daddy said, "Looks like roman candles, don't it?"

For the next half hour, we circled the fire, pushing the longer branches in as their twiggy tops burned away. It was hot, sweaty work, but the flames kept our clothes dry. The smell of green leaves burning was unbearably nostalgic. Most of the time, I'm an adult, able to bear what has to be borne with an adult's stoicism. But there are times when I miss Mother so much it's like a physical hurt that's never healed. She used to love bonfires, too.

Eventually, as the fire settled down, we sat on a nearby fallen log, talking of nothing important, watching the fire burn lower.

Without really thinking, I said, "You paying John Claude to represent the Love boy?"

He didn't answer.

"You're still messing with whiskey, aren't you?"

There was such a long silence that I was almost afraid that I'd made him really mad. On the other hand, if he *is* still bootlegging, it threatens my professional reputation.

At last he said, "Your mama never understood why I couldn't leave it alone. She thought it was the whiskey itself, but it won't. You never seen me drunk, did you?"

"No, sir."

"No, it won't the whiskey. And after a while, it won't even the money."

Another silence.

"What, then?" I asked.

"I guess you might say it was the excitement. Running the risks. Knowing what I could lose if I got caught. That's something your mama never rightly understood."

He turned and looked at me a long level moment by

the dying fire. "You understand though, don't you, shug?"

Now it was my turn to sit silently.

He nodded and poked the fire again. Another burst of bright sparks gushed upward in swirls of red and gold against the night sky.

Through the ravaged trees to the north, an answering glow suddenly appeared, a brilliant whiteness against the treetops.

It was the floodlights of a power crew working its way into the dark countryside.